FINDERS REAPERS

NEW ORLEANS

NOCTURNES

CARRIE PULKINEN

Finders Reapers

Contact Information: www.CarriePulkinen.com

Cover Art by Rebecca Poole of Dreams2Media
Edited by Krista Venero of Mountains Wanted

First Edition, 2020
ISBN: 978-1-7347624-1-9

The grim reaper took a vacation.
Now all hell is breaking loose.

With an existential crisis looming over his head, Asher needs a break from reaping souls. But when he leaves his door to the underworld unattended, one escaped ghost threatens to turn the French Quarter into a haven for the hell-bound.

Oh, and that crisis he was trying to escape? Her name is Jasmine Lee, and she could be the death of him.

The literal death of Death. Yep. You heard that right.

There's no such thing as too dead when it comes to necromancer Jasmine Lee. She's never met a ghost she can't tame, but when a thousand ornery spirits descend upon New Orleans, her secret weakness is a recipe for phantasmal disaster.

Holy ghost guts. She's in trouble.

The unfairly hot reaper is the last person Jasmine wants to work with. But if she doesn't help Asher wrangle the lost souls back to the underworld, there will be hell to pay.

Literally.

Enjoy a smoldering brush with Death in this fast, fun romantic comedy.

CHAPTER ONE

"Don't worry. Corpses can't feel pain." Jasmine Lee flashed her most comforting smile at the nauseated werewolf. "Once the life force leaves the body, the synapses are kaput. You couldn't get on this dude's nerves if you wanted to."

She paused, waiting for Jax to crack a smile, but tension rolled through the poor guy's body, and the look on his face said he was either about to blow chunks or bolt. Shifting her gaze to Trace, the other werewolf standing with them in the morgue, she grinned. He shook his head.

"Oh, come on. Shifters have no appreciation for morgue humor." She gestured to the metal bin against the wall. "There's a trash can if you need it. Trace did his first time."

A low growl rumbled in Trace's chest. At least *that* comment got a response.

"A chunk of his neck is missing." Jax swallowed hard and inched a little closer to the corpse covered in a sheet.

"How could he possibly not feel it when you shove his soul back into his mangled body?"

Jasmine sighed. "Synapses kaput? Dead nerves? I thought I explained this already."

"Let's get it over with." Trace wiggled a finger toward the top of the sheet. "If it's a dog bite like the coroner claims, we'll be on our way. If a shifter did this, we'll have a mess of trouble on our hands."

"As you wish, Officer." When she grasped the sheet, she could practically feel Jax tensing. Seriously, you could have cracked a walnut between the dude's butt cheeks. Watching him out of the corner of her eye, she uncovered the top half of the corpse. The stiff was in his late twenties with short, light brown hair, and though his skin held the ashy pallor of death, he looked like he might have had a tan in life.

Jax's stomach heaved, but he kept his dinner down. Not bad for a first-timer.

"Naturally, the coroner doesn't know y'all exist, so he's calling it a dog bite. It happened on a sidewalk in the Garden District in the middle of the night, so no witnesses."

Trace leaned closer to the body, holding his breath as he peered at the wound. Jasmine was all but nose blind to the scents of death now, but werewolves' heightened sense of smell made coming to the morgue a stomach-turning event for all of them. "Those are teeth marks, but it's impossible to tell if a shifter did this or just an animal. We need to talk to him."

She bowed formally. "Jasmine Lee, necromancer extraordinaire, at your service. There's no such thing as too dead when it comes to me. Did you know there's never been a soul I couldn't call back from across the bridge?"

She paused and tilted her head. "Let me clarify, there's never been a soul I couldn't grab that didn't make a deal with the Devil before they died. If Satan owns them, no one can call them back, so those people don't really count."

Those were the ones she had to catch before that damn, meddling, unfairly hot reaper snatched them away and ferried them off to the underworld. He'd ripped one too many souls from her grasp, making a mockery of her in front of her employers, and she would never forgive him for that.

Trace cleared his throat.

"Right. Focus, Jazz." She shook her arms, loosening herself up to make the connection with the other side. "Y'all ready for this?"

"As we'll ever be," Jax said through clenched teeth.

Jasmine took a deep breath, opening her channel to the spirit world. Her chest warmed, a sensation not unlike heartburn tightening beneath her breastbone, but instead of the burning, fizzing feeling reaching upward like she'd eaten a pound of extra-spicy crawfish, it descended into her stomach, filling her core with warm, effervescent magic.

Placing her hand on the dead guy's forehead, she absorbed his essence and shuffled through the energy of the spirit world, searching for his soul. "Oh, this is too easy. He hasn't even crossed the bridge yet."

In her mind, she reached out, clutching the energy that matched the body and shoving it into the corpse. There was no gentle way to do this. She'd tried delicately placing the soul on top of the body, allowing it to seep in slowly in the hope of minimizing the shock for her patients.

It never worked. The only way to fuse a soul with a corpse was to shove it in there like an angry housewife stuffing a turkey while her mother-in-law stood behind her, criticizing her every move.

With the spirit firmly planted inside the body, she stepped back and waited. This was the exciting part. First, the eyes moved beneath the lids like he was dreaming. Then, they flew open as he attempted to suck in his first breath of air since he died. Of course, the lungs didn't work anymore, and he was dead, so he had no need for oxygen. But the body responded, mimicking the movements of breathing.

The dead guy lay there, staring at the ceiling and blinking. Jasmine followed his gaze to find plain, white ceiling tiles and plastic, rectangular panels covering fluorescent lights. What a drab thing for a stiff to see on his first reanimation. Maybe she could convince the coroner to let her commission an artist to paint a mural on the ceiling. Or maybe she could hang a sign like on *The Good Place* that read, "Welcome! Everything is fine!"

Except everything wasn't fine, because the deceased would go back to being dead as soon as whoever was using her services got the information they needed.

The stiff lifted an arm, pressing it against his neck wound as he attempted to sit up. Jasmine placed a firm hand on his shoulder. "Probably best if you stay down, buddy. I'm not sure your head'll stay attached if you move."

One eye rolled toward Jasmine before the other caught up. Dead bodies were weird like that. It took time for a spirit to gain the ability to move a corpse convincingly, and this guy wouldn't be sticking around long enough to master it.

"What happened?" An icky, sloshing sound came from the wound when he spoke, and Jax gagged.

Jasmine held in a laugh as the big, bad werewolf turned green, eyeing the trash can like his last meal was about to make a reappearance. It was a dead body, for goodness' sake; it was going to make noises. These guys hunted in their wolf forms, using their mouths to tear apart the flesh of whatever poor animal they caught for dinner, yet they freaked out at the sight of a talking corpse. *Sheesh.*

"We were hoping you could tell us what happened." She moved closer so he could see her without turning his head too far. "You were attacked, and you died. Do you remember anything?"

"I couldn't find the light." Panic laced his words. "I've been roaming around the streets, but no one can see me. Aren't I supposed to go to heaven now?"

"You're supposed to go somewhere, but that's not for us to decide. If you can't cross the bridge on your own, I'm sure a reaper will be along soon to show you the way."

There were three reasons a ghost might hang around in the aether, the metaphysical space between the earthly realm and the underworld. Some simply got lost and couldn't find their way. If that were the case for this guy, Asher—the sexy-as-sin reaper whom Jasmine *hated*—would find him and whisk him away. Others had misbehaved in life, and rather than being tortured in hell, their spirits were forced to roam the Earth as punishment. The last bunch had unfinished business with the living. They'd hang around until their murder was solved or they got their revenge or made peace with whomever they were at odds with…whatever it took.

Jasmine had no way of knowing this dude's fate, so all

she could do was promise him he'd get what was coming to him when the time was right. It wouldn't have surprised her if the reaper showed up that instant, snatching the soul away before the werewolves got the information they needed, not saying a word to her when he did it. That was typical Asher style ever since *the incident*...the thing that happened between them that she refused to think about anymore.

They used to be friends. Good friends. She'd *thought* their friendship was turning into something more until he freaked out and…

She clenched her teeth. Memory lane was a dead-end street she did not need to go skipping down right now. "Don't worry, buddy. It'll all work out. Now, what do you remember about your death? What attacked you? Was it a wolf?"

"No baiting the witness," Trace grumbled.

Jasmine rolled her eyes. "This isn't a courtroom. Sometimes the dead need a little help remembering."

"It was my girlfriend's new Rottweiler. She got it a few days after she dumped me." The stiff turned his head toward Jasmine, and his bones crunched, making yellow-tinged goo leak from the gash in his neck.

"Oh, hell." Jax lunged for the trash can and heaved.

Jasmine shook her head. *Wimp.* "You're sure it was a Rottweiler?"

"Yeah. We'd broken up a week before. I was sneaking around to make sure she hadn't hooked up with anyone else. When I opened the gate, the dog came barreling toward me and latched onto my neck. I fell backward, and I guess I hit my head. That's all I remember."

She looked at Trace. "Got what you needed?"

"Yeah. Thanks, Jasmine. You know where to send the

bill." He nodded and turned to Jax, who stood doubled over the trash can.

"Don't let him turn around. This is the icky part." Jasmine waited until Trace put his hand on Jax's back, and she focused her energy on the soul inside the corpse. "Thanks for your help, buddy. I'm gonna send you back to the aether now."

"What's going to happen to me?" His voice trembled, though she couldn't tell if it was from fear or because he was decaying. "Where will I go?"

"Like I said, if you can't find the light, look for the reaper. He's a tall, blond guy. Fair skin, otherworldly hotness. You can't miss him. Otherwise, just hang out. You're dead now, so no more pain. That's a bonus, right?"

He started to speak again, so Jasmine placed her hand on his forehead and yanked the soul from his body. The corpse seized, the torso shaking and the limbs flailing like it was given an electric shock, while the gentle buzzing of magic in Jasmine's core turned to a sharp zap of pain.

The moment the spirit was free of the body, she pushed it out of the room. The sensation in her abdomen dissipated, and thus ended the semi-lifelike state the corpse had endured. The dude lay still as a...well, as a corpse.

"My job is done here." Jasmine arranged the limbs onto the tray like they'd been before, covered the dead guy's head, and slid the locker shut. "Thanks for visiting the meat library, boys. Wanna go grab a drink?" She took off her lab coat and washed her hands.

Jax's face contorted like he was about to be sick again. "After what I just saw? No thanks."

"I've got to get home to Sophie." Trace opened the door. "Maybe next time."

"Sure. Yeah. No problem." Jasmine waved as they shot out of the morgue faster than a couple of vampires who'd just drained a caffeine addict.

With a sigh, she cleaned up the mess, checking the handle on the locker she'd closed to be sure it was secure. Technically, she was nothing more than a research assistant at the morgue. Only the other supes and the higher-ups in the police force knew about her "side gig" as a necromancer, and she intended to keep it that way. After scanning the room for any traces of supernatural evidence, she turned off the lights on her way out the door.

She shouldn't have expected either of the guys to take her up on her offer of grabbing a drink. Anyone who knew about her powers—which meant virtually *all* supes—steered a wide berth around her. With her connection to the dead, and her ability to command them, everyone assumed she lived with one foot on Earth and one in the underworld.

In reality, she'd never been to the underworld and had no plans to visit the place until her own soul was summoned to whatever realm of the dead her deeds in life earned her. Seeing and talking to ghosts didn't bother most supes, but her ability to call people back from across the bridge and to reanimate corpses creeped everyone out.

Well, almost everyone.

Demons didn't mind her abilities, but most of them were despicable. And vampires... She was like supernatural catnip to the bloodsuckers. Her power to command the dead was a turn on to them for some strange reason. Probably because their own souls were so loosely attached to their undead bodies that they were *dying* to be set free. And her magic had her itching to help them along. More than one vamp had turned into a stalker when she'd tried to be friends, so now she stayed as far away as possible to avoid the unnatural attraction.

Then there was Asher.

She'd thought he, of all people, would be able to accept her, but nope. The moment their friendship got the teensiest bit romantic, he dropped her like a lava rock from the bowels of hell and never spoke to her again.

Was it too much to ask for someone—*anyone*, supe, human, she didn't care—to accept her, morbid abilities and all? Most women her age were getting married and starting families, something it seemed Jasmine would never get to do. She smiled sadly. She and Asher could have made some beautiful babies together.

But it didn't matter. He'd treated their friendship like he treated souls, tossing it into a pit and never looking back. Who did that to people? A dick, that's who.

She tugged the door shut and spun around, gasping as she stepped right through the dead guy's ghost. The frigid spirit ripped through her torso, clawing at her skin with icy fingers until she jumped out of the way.

That's what it felt like anyway. Really, the ghost was just as shocked as she was. He looked at her quizzically, gripping his arms as if checking that everything was still in place.

Jasmine shook off the chilling sensation and adjusted the purse strap on her shoulder. "Still can't find the light, huh?"

"No one can. We don't know what to do."

"We? So you've found some other spirits? That's a good thing. Y'all can hang out together until it's time to go."

As she continued down the hall toward the building exit, her phone buzzed in her pocket.

She pulled it out and groaned at the screen. A text

from her sister read: *Where the hell are you, Jazz? Don't make me endure this alone.*

"Crap. That was tonight?" She'd completely forgotten about her cousin's bachelorette party. *Ugh. Even a spoiled brat like Raina can find love.*

She typed her response: *Sorry. Tell her I had to work late. On my way.* Then she shoved the phone in her pocket. The human side of her family—her mom's side—wasn't in the know about supes and thought Jasmine and her sister Ella were simple psychics. *More like weirdos.* She couldn't exactly tell them she was busy raising the dead.

The ghost dude floated by her side. "There's something wrong. We're all stuck here."

"Stuck?" Jasmine paused, and the spirit hovered next to her, so close his death chill seeped into her arm.

Fun fact: necromancers could communicate with the dead much more efficiently than mediums, but there was a reason they preferred to reanimate corpses rather than deal with the spirits directly. If she spent too long with a ghost in close proximity, it could drain her energy, increasing its own strength while sucking the life out of her.

Spend too long with *too* many of them, and she'd become a ghost herself. Dead as an antique doorknocker. Gotta love that kind of irony, right?

The weakness was kept in strict confidence among the necromancers; they couldn't let the mediums think they were better than them. Necromancers were way more powerful than any run-of-the-mill psychic. But great strength was always balanced by great weakness. It was the natural order of things. Like vampires turning to barbecue in the sun.

"There's no light to go to. Everyone says the door is

locked." The dead dude reached for her, and she jumped backward like a werewolf peeing on an electric fence.

"Whoa. Back up, buddy. No touching." She raised her hands and waited for the ghost to float away. "First off, what's your name again? Camden? Carter?" She'd looked him up when Trace requested her services, but she tried not to get too attached to the dead. Names were personal, so she shoved them out of her mind as soon as she was done with her work.

"It's Cameron."

"Cameron, right. Can I call you Cam?" She didn't wait for his response. "What the hell are you talking about, Cam? The door is never locked. You either can't find it, or you aren't meant to go through it yet."

Where was that damn reaper when she needed him? Ever since *the incident,* Asher seemed to have a knack for reaping the souls she required and leaving the annoying clingers behind to torture her.

"I swear, it's locked. Please, can you help?"

She rubbed at the goosebumps on her arms. "I don't know anything about a door. I imagine the line between the world of the dead and here as a bridge, and it's always open for business."

Sadness filled Cameron's eyes, and the poor guy looked so pathetic, she actually felt sorry for him. It wasn't her job to help spirits pass on, but...

Sighing, she shook her head. She was probably going to regret this. "Okay. I'll talk to the reaper for you and see if he knows what's up with your door, but you've got to keep your distance. You keep sucking my warmth away, and the deal's off. Got it?"

He nodded.

"Good. Now, make yourself scarce. I'll call you when I

talk to him." She passed through the door to the reception area, and thankfully, Cameron didn't follow. After she signed out and said goodbye to the front desk clerk, she leaned a hip against the release bar and pushed open the front door.

Jasmine stopped dead in her tracks.

Well, not really dead; she was alive and kickin', but the swarm of ghosts waiting for her in the parking lot froze her to the spot. There had to be at least thirty spirits hovering around the morgue, and all their gazes were trained on her. She swallowed hard.

This was a necromancer's nightmare.

CHAPTER TWO

A warm, salty wave crashed over Asher's head a second before the riptide yanked him beneath the surface, spitting him out ten yards farther from shore. He gasped as he cleared another wave, sucking in as much oxygen as possible before diving deep and powering toward the coastline.

Kicking his legs as hard as he could, he finally made it to the shallows and stood, panting with exhaustion. *Satan's balls.* Reapers might be immortal, but that sea nearly kicked his ass. No wonder the humans had put up a no swimming sign and hung a red flag from the deserted lifeguard stand.

Trudging through the water toward the beach, he eyed the warning sign he'd blatantly ignored. He'd been following the rules his entire life, trying his damnedest to be a good little soldier like the other reapers and bottling up the emotions he wasn't supposed to feel.

He still felt them, though, and that was part of his problem. A problem he came here to ignore, and with the sand beneath his toes and the salt in his hair, he would continue *not* thinking about it for as long as he could.

With a contented sigh, he lay back in the lounge chair he'd reserved and sipped the pineapple daiquiri that sat waiting for him after his swim. July in Aruba was the off season, which meant the small resort he'd booked was nearly empty. The secluded beach sat deserted, just the way he liked it, and he closed his eyes, basking in the heat of the sun and the sound of the crystal blue waves crashing into the shore.

This vacation was exactly what he needed to relax for a while and forget about the existential crisis looming over his head. Hell, he'd been working nonstop for the past two-hundred-something years, and after his romantic screw-up—and the unsettling revelation that arose from it —he *had* to get away.

His life was on the line, after all, and that meant a lot for an immortal being.

He deserved a break, and since Charon, the man in charge of the reapers' schedules, didn't offer a benefits package, Asher did the only thing he could and went AWOL.

Why the idea of just up and leaving hadn't struck him before, he wasn't sure. But ever since he helped a witch make it to Satan's palace—despite the fact she'd been struck from the list of souls to deliver—he'd realized some-thing most reapers hadn't.

Rules *could* be broken.

Crimson had made a deal to become the Devil's personal assistant. Asher was supposed to deliver her body and soul to the palace, but the moment he opened the portal and took her through his door into the underworld, her name disappeared from his roster. It seemed her demon boyfriend Mike—Asher's best friend—had struck his own deal to save Crimson from hell.

At that point, Asher should have shoved her back through the door onto Earth, but he didn't. Crimson had been convinced Mike was in trouble, and Asher couldn't let his best friend suffer. So, he took her through the underworld and delivered her to Satan's doorstep, thumbing his nose at the possibility of being thrown in the tarpits for disobeying rule number one: never bring a living soul into hell.

He'd broken a cardinal rule, and he'd gotten away with it.

If he could pull that off, a two-week vacation would be a piece of cake.

Speaking of cake, the resort restaurant had a delectable German chocolate masterpiece on the dessert menu. Maybe he should treat himself to one more slice before he hit the shower. Chocolate made everything better. He set his daiquiri on the little table next to his sun lounger and swung his legs over the side of the seat.

As he started to stand, a portal opened above the adjacent lounger, and a man with white hair and turquoise eyes appeared on the chair. He wore the standard-issue black robes of a reaper—which Asher reserved for only the orneriest of spirits—and a sprinkling of freckles dotted his pale cheeks. "I thought I sensed another reaper in my territory. Are you here for training?"

Asher blinked, mildly offended this guy would think he, a two-hundred-something year veteran—he'd lost count after his two-hundred-tenth birthday—would need training, but more perturbed at the reminder of the duties he was shirking.

Shirk, schmirk. Even criminals got time off for good behavior.

"Sorry to intrude." Reapers' solitary nature could make them a bit territorial. Now that he thought about it, he'd never sensed another reaper in his own territory in his entire existence. Aside from their trips to hell and back, they didn't travel much. "I'm on vacation. Now, if you'll excuse me, there's a piece of cake with my name on it waiting in the restaurant."

"A reaper on vacation. Now there's an interesting concept." He folded his hands behind his head and stretched out on the lounger. "You were literally made to reap souls, yet you're taking a break from it?" He shook his head. "I can't imagine that. It would be like a shifter who stopped shifting, or a human who actually fact-checked before they shared a social media post. Unnatural."

Asher ground his teeth and leaned back in his chair. The man had a point. Sure, he'd felt an emptiness inside ever since he'd arrived at the resort, but he didn't think it was because he missed reaping. He'd chalked it up to missing a certain necromancer he'd had his eye on for the past year or so.

And the fact he'd had his eye on a *necromancer* was the root of all his problems.

Asher knew he was an anomaly. Though he considered himself antisocial compared to his friends, having friends at all indicated he wasn't like the other reapers. He hadn't seen any of his eight brothers and sisters in more than a hundred years, and his parents…

If he were honest with himself, what happened to his parents scared him the most. His mom was a reaper. She'd lived six hundred years when she fell in love with a necromancer—Asher's dad—and she'd been happy. She'd bubbled with joy in every memory Asher had of her, but necromancers weren't immortal like reapers, and falling in love tied their fates. When his father passed away, his mother followed shortly after.

It was the reason so few reapers existed. The only beings capable of loving them—of having a family with them—were powerful necromancers, and falling in love meant becoming mortal. Sure, he'd have the chance of expanding his kind's population, thus lightening the work-load on everyone, but the cost…

He'd known he was falling for Jasmine as their friend-ship bloomed, and he could handle his own feelings, bottling them up like he always had. But when she admitted she liked him back, the weight of what was happening threatened to drown him. It seemed he was following in his mother's footsteps, and that, he didn't know how to handle.

He didn't want to die.

So he ran. He avoided Jasmine as much as he could, but when she started summoning the souls he needed to reap, he ran again.

Now, here he was, sharing the beach and the longest conversation he'd ever had with a reaper—aside from his family—with a guy he'd just met.

"My name's Augustus, by the way, but you can call me Gus. Nice to meet you." He inclined his head but didn't offer his hand.

"I'm Asher."

Gus stared out over the water, a silence stretching between them that grated on Asher's nerves like sand-paper on a sunburn. Reapers weren't known for their conversational prowess, and that cake wasn't going to eat itself.

He was just about to portal out of there when Gus finally spoke. "Where's your territory?"

"New Orleans. Well...all of Louisiana, but I live in New Orleans." He sucked down the rest of his daiquiri and set the empty glass on the table.

Gus nodded. "Now it makes sense. You live topside with the humans, don't you?"

He shrugged. "Yeah. It's a great place to live."

"Were you assigned to stay topside, or did you request it?" His tone held a hint of accusation.

"It was offered, and I agreed."

Sitting up, Gus turned to face him, giving him an "oh, you're *that* reaper" look. That once every three-hundred years abnormality who actually liked people. That creature of Death who'd be willing to give up his immortality and die.

No, he wasn't *that* reaper. Not by choice anyway.

"You know humans invented the whole idea of vacations, right? Lazy bastards. Sounds like they're rubbing off on you."

"That's impossible." Asher hardly associated with the humans. Hell, he barely had any supe friends because people who knew what he was tended to think their lives were in jeopardy if they got too close to him—which couldn't be further from the truth.

Sure, he had the ability to sever souls from the living, but he only did it when the soul in question had been sold to Satan, and it was time to give the Devil his due. Otherwise, he was completely harmless.

"Is it?" Gus glanced at him before staring out over the water again. "How'd you pull it off, anyway? With a territory that big, it seems like it would be overrun with ghosts by now."

"I thought it all through before I left." He wasn't *so* irresponsible that he'd leave his job with no plan in place to usher the souls to the underworld. "I infused a bowl with my magic, so the tithes will appear when the spirits arrive. And since humans always think they need to look for 'the light' when they die, I installed a porch light over my door to the underworld to magnify the natural glow."

Gus arched a brow. "That's your solution? A porch light?" He laughed. "You may have made yourself obsolete, my friend."

"Not just any light. I convinced a sun fairy to travel through my portal and infuse the bulb with magical UV light. Now my door is like a lighthouse in a fog. A beacon for the dead. No one in Louisiana will get lost in the haze of death again."

"Are you insane?" Gus shot upright, planting his feet in the sand. "You put fairy light in the underworld? The light of a *sun* fairy...on your unlocked door?"

"Well, if I locked it, the light wouldn't do much good would it? I'd go home to find a horde of ghosts trying to knock down the door like some zombie movie."

"Did you stop to think that kind of light might attract the souls from the *other* side of the door? Ones that want to escape?"

"I..." Asher's heart sank. He hadn't thought of that. "Charon wouldn't give them passage to The Rock. There's no way a soul could cross the River Styx without his ferry." Every reaper's door led to the same place: a massive boulder in the underworld with the River Styx raging all around it. If a soul fell into the river, it would be boiled for all eternity. Charon ferried the souls from The Rock to the mainland for processing—a one-way trip.

"It wouldn't be the first time a soul of the damned

escaped. And you know what happens to your door if a spirit uses it as an exit."

"It locks." *Oh, shit.*

Gus nodded. "No one gets in or out, including you." He rose to his feet. "But I'm sure someone will contact you if there's a problem. Enjoy your vacation." With a wave of his arm, he opened a portal and stepped through, leaving Asher alone on the beach with nothing but his racing heart and churning stomach for company.

Everything was fine. There was nothing to worry about. He kept telling himself that as he scrambled through the sand toward his room. Yanking open the sliding glass door, he darted inside and fumbled to turn on his phone. He'd powered it down the moment he arrived in Aruba and hadn't used the damn thing since.

As the screen illuminated, a notification pinged. Then another, and another. Name after name scrolled across his screen so quickly he couldn't read a word. The incessant chime sounded again and again until it became one long, solid *beeeeeeeeeeep*.

The screen blinked, the image distorting as if it were made of paint and someone zigzagged their finger through. With a zap, it went black.

"Oh, no." Asher furiously tapped the glass with his index finger, but it didn't refresh. He held down the power button, but it wouldn't turn back on. Whatever was happening in New Orleans had overloaded his phone, shorting the circuits and the magic, rendering it useless.

He could only hope the same thing hadn't happened to the city.

CHAPTER THREE

Jasmine activated her protection magic, creating an energy bubble around herself to keep the spirits out. Upon closer inspection, her original estimate of the number of ghosts swarming her seemed bloated, but could you blame her? Even the ten or fifteen waiting for her in the parking lot would give the most mundane human a serious case of the heebie-jeebies.

"Hay, Cam?" She sifted through the spirit energy and found the dead guy's essence, dragging him toward her. "What in hell's name is going on? Did you organize this?"

Cam lowered his head. "You're a necromancer. I thought you could help."

Time worked differently for the dead, but damn. It had taken the guy all of thirty living seconds to gather a gaggle of ghosts, and he'd only been dead a day! He shouldn't have been that powerful. Not yet.

As the ghosts drifted toward her, enclosing her in a semicircle of death, Jasmine threw up her hands and sent out a pulse of magic. "Y'all need to back off."

The spirits jumped backward like they'd been struck

with an electrical current, which they had, and their postures straightened like soldiers standing at attention.

"That's more like it." Jasmine stepped forward, opening her arms to her sides, parting the ghosts to make a path she could pass through. "I understand you've got some problems. Cameron said your door is locked. Is that right?"

"Not just locked." A female spirit in a delivery company uniform floated forward. "The light has been extinguished. It was shining so brightly, but I stopped to say goodbye to my husband before I went to it. By the time I was done, it had burned out."

Jasmine crossed her arms, eyeing the woman. "Just because you can't find it doesn't mean it's not there. Sometimes spirits have unfinished business here on Earth."

"I can't find it either," a teenage boy said.

"Neither can I…" All of the ghosts joined in, claiming they couldn't find the light.

Cameron arched a ghostly brow. "Told you."

"Yeah, you did." She strode toward her Prius parked in the lot.

"Where are you going?" Cameron followed after her. "You said you'd help."

"And I will." She yanked open the door and slid into the driver's seat. "But right now, I've got business to attend to with the living, and if I don't get my ass there soon, my sister's going to make sure I become one of you. I'll find you when I figure out what's happening."

The ghosts disappeared, and Jasmine ground her teeth as she searched for Asher's number in her contacts. She was loath to call the man, but what choice did she have? She certainly couldn't find the magical doorway souls passed through to the underworld—nor did she have any desire to.

Holding her breath, she dialed the number, but the call went straight to voicemail. *Figures.* "Asher, it's Jasmine. Where the hell are you, dude? There's a bunch of ghosts who claim they can't find your light, which apparently means your door is locked. What gives? Are they all being punished for something, or is there a problem? Not that I care about your problems, but these spirits are encroaching on my personal space, and I'd rather you—"

"Mailbox full," a chipper female computer voice said into her ear.

"Dammit." Jasmine tossed her phone into her purse and made her way toward the French Quarter. The dead couldn't get any deader, so they could wait. Her sister, however, could not. By now, Ella probably wanted to kill her, so unless Jasmine wanted to join the horde of dearly departed, she had to get a move on.

———

Asher checked out of the hotel before taking his suitcase into the restroom and tearing a hole through reality. Stepping through the portal into his apartment, he dropped his bag on the floor and rerouted the gateway to take him to hell.

But his portal wouldn't open all the way to the underworld.

Instead of spilling him out onto The Rock like it usually did, his wormhole to another dimension ended in total darkness. He stumbled over the rocky terrain until he face-planted into something solid. The impact jarred his skull, but as he recovered, he ran his hands over the surface, tracing the outline of a door.

His door.

His own magic tingled on his fingers as he felt along the edges for the knob. He wrapped his hand around the cool, celestial metal and gave it a twist. It didn't budge. "C'mon. I made you; you have to open for me."

He jiggled it, twisting to the right and then the left. Still nothing happened. "Oh, I know what the problem is." He chuckled and patted the door as if it were an old friend. It had been two weeks. The threshold probably didn't recognize him in his human form.

Fishing in his pocket, he pulled out his I Heart NOLA pen filled with purple and green glitter and clicked the button on the end. In a flash of silver light, the pen elongated into a six-foot-long scythe with a wicked-sharp blade, and he unleashed his reaper magic, his body buzzing with electricity as he transformed from a muscular, blond-haired, blue-eyed man in jeans and a t-shirt to a skeletal being in a black robe.

Damn it felt good to be himself. He hadn't shed his skin in weeks, and while he enjoyed living topside, sometimes it was nice to let it all hang out. He could never show his true self to the humans. Hell, most supes would shit their pants if they saw him like this. He'd never killed anyone in his entire existence—aside from taking the bartered souls to Satan when he called for them—but when you look like the embodiment of Death itself, your reputation precedes you. Every. Where. You. Go.

He looked at his door, giving it a moment to soak in his true form, and then he tried the knob again. It didn't turn.

"Satan's balls," he grumbled as he tried to force the

damn thing open, slamming his shoulder against the wood. Nothing.

"Alright. If you want to play that way." Gripping his scythe in both hands, he swung the blade at the knob. The impact reverberated up the handle, jarring his joints and making him madder than a hornet whose nest was sprayed with bug killer.

With a grunt, he swung the scythe again. Never mind the fact the blade was forged to sever souls from their connection to the earthly plane; it was sharper than a sasquatch's razor and should have sliced right through the door.

Instead, as metal hit metal, sparks ignited, lighting up the darkness and sending Asher flying backward through his portal. He landed on his ass in the middle of his living room topside, and the scythe bounced off the floor, the blade lodging in the wall with a *thunk*.

He activated his glamour, returning to his human form before jumping to his feet and retrieving the tool. With a tap of his finger, it transformed back into an ink pen, and he shoved it in his pocket. He'd deal with the hole in the drywall later.

Laughter sounded from the sidewalk below, and he peered out the window to find a group of tourists walking by. Vibrant ferns overflowed their pots on the gallery across the street, and a sidewalk musician stopped to chug a bottle of water in the summer heat before picking up his violin and continuing his song.

A block over, three spirits hovered on the street corner, their gazes searching the air around them like they were looking for something they couldn't find.

Life went on, but the dead were stuck, thanks to Asher's idiotic plan to take an unauthorized vacation. *This* was why he'd been following the rules for two-hundred-something years. What made him think breaking them would be a good idea now?

Reapers reaped souls. They followed an ancient code of conduct, obeyed the rules, did their jobs, and the world ran smoothly. Asher was no different. He didn't *want* to be different because no good ever came from miscreancy.

Now, the magical door that allowed the dead to pass into the underworld was locked, just as he feared, and there was only one way to fix it. He had to find the spirit who used his entrance as an exit. The question was, who had escaped?

Jasmine's arm hairs stood on end as she waited for the bouncer to check her ID. She'd scored a parking spot in the lot next door and hurried across the street before any more ghosts could get in her way. Now if this guy would just hurry up...

With a grunt, he handed the plastic card back to her, allowing her access to the club, and she shoved her license into her purse. A blast of cold air chilled her skin when she stepped through the door, and thumping bass vibrated in her chest as she ventured deeper into the room.

A disco ball hung in the center of the dance floor, while booths lined the walls and tables dotted the rest of the floor in the dimly lit bar. People danced and mingled, and Jasmine took a deep breath, steeling herself for the night to come.

"There you are. What took you so long?" Her sister Ella took her arm and dragged her toward the party. She wore a hot pink t-shirt with zebra print writing, but Jasmine didn't catch what it said.

"Sorry." She scanned the room to be sure none of the ghostly mob from the parking lot had followed her inside. Usually, her word was law when it came to the dead, but something in the air outside felt different.

Okay, law might not have been the right word. It wasn't like she wore a robe and a powdered wig when she told spirits what to do, but they did tend to listen. Necromancers could control the dead...up to a point. Hopefully telling fifteen spirits to leave her alone until she talked to Asher didn't cross the line.

Speaking of Asher... She tugged her phone from her pocket, but he hadn't returned her call. *Typical.*

"Are you okay?" Ella stopped by a table and grabbed a rolled-up piece of pink fabric. "Hold on. You forgot about tonight, didn't you?" Her eyes narrowed accusingly.

"I... No! I was just—"

"We shared a womb, Jazz. I can tell when you're lying." Ella shoved the fabric toward her.

"It also helps that you're an empath," she grumbled as she unrolled the shirt and shook it out. While Jasmine inherited her father's necromancy ability, Ella was like a psychic on steroids. Her uncanny ability to read the emotions of anyone in a half-mile radius made her almost clairvoyant.

Ella grinned. "That helps too. But, seriously, sis. You seem off today. Everything alright?"

"Yeah, fine. I made an appointment at the fertility clinic for a week from Thursday. You're still going to drive me, right?"

"You're serious about going through with that?"

"I'm twenty-eight, and I'm not growing younger. I want to have children."

Sympathy softened her sister's eyes. "Are you sure you don't want to wait until Mr. Right comes along?"

"By the time that happens—*if* it happens at all—I'll be too old. I'm just freezing my eggs right now. I'll decide how to use them later."

"Of course." Ella nodded. "You know I'll be there."

Jasmine grimaced at the matching t-shirt her sister had handed her. The zebra print writing read *The SHE to my nanigans,* and an arrow pointed to the left. Ella's arrow pointed the opposite direction. "She can't expect us all to stand on the correct sides of her all night."

"She can, and she does. Now put it on before she notices how late her favorite cousin is to her bachelorette party."

Jasmine snorted and pulled the shirt over her head. "Favorite? That's funny."

"Look who's here." Ella tugged her toward the bride's tribe, and their cousin Raina looked down her nose at Jasmine.

"How was work?" Raina asked. "Busy, I guess?"

"Oh, it's always dead there." Jasmine smirked, and Ella snickered.

Raina crossed her arms. "If it was dead, why were you late?"

Jasmine's brow rose as she waited for her words to sink in. When Raina simply blinked, she responded, "It's dead because I work at *the morgue.*"

Ella laughed. "That one never gets old. I love your *killer* puns."

"I don't get it." Raina titled her head.

"Have another shot." Ella tugged their cousin toward a

table and offered her a glass, while Jasmine let out a sigh of relief.

Her sister was so much better with people than she was. Judging by social skills alone, it was hard to believe they were even related, much less twins. Jasmine turned toward the bar in search of her own libation, and her gaze landed on her best friend, Katrina.

"You have no idea how happy I am to see you." Jasmine strode toward her and slid onto a stool. "Are you here alone?"

Katrina handed her a bottle of Abita Amber and gave her a quizzical look. "I'm here for you."

"How did you know I needed you? Do your demon senses work like that?" She took a long sip of the beer, reveling in the way the icy bubbles cooled her throat.

"Uh...you asked me to meet you here?" She pressed a hand to Jasmine's forehead. "Are you feeling okay?"

"You're the second person to ask me that tonight." Truth was, she did feel a bit rattled after seeing all those ghosts. In fact, she'd felt *off* for the past week and a half or so, but she'd chalked it up to stress.

She checked her phone again, her shoulders slumping at the blank screen. "Have you seen Asher around lately?"

Katrina cocked a brow as a knowing smile curved her red lips. "Is someone pining over a hot-as-sin reaper who won't return her calls?"

Jasmine's lip curled. "No. Absolutely not." *Not anymore.*

"Don't take it personally. Reapers are solitary creatures. Asher's an oddity in that he lives topside with the rest of us. Most of them create a void in the aether and hang out there when they're not working."

Katrina smoothed her dark brown hair back into her

ponytail. "Before you ask, I have not sampled him. Reapers aren't my type."

"I didn't realize succubi had types."

"When you can have anyone you want, you develop preferences. If I weren't fasting, I'd be going after a tall, dark, and handsome. Reapers are much too pale."

Jasmine shook her head. "Good to know, but you never answered my question. Have you seen him?"

"Not in the past couple of weeks, now that you mention it. Why? Did he ghost you?"

Jasmine laughed, but Katrina didn't seem to get her own joke. *Ghosting* a necromancer? That was funny.

She was about to explain the mob that ambushed her outside the morgue when Ella sashayed toward them with a shot glass in her hand. Her sister tipped her head back and downed the blue liquid before wrapping an arm around Jasmine's shoulders. "It's too early for you to ditch the group."

"You seem to be getting along fine." She took her sister's glass—which was currently leaking syrupy alcohol onto her arm—and set it on the bar.

"When in Rome, you know? C'mon. We need a group picture before everyone has drunk eyes."

"Drunk eyes?" Katrina inquired.

"When humans get tipsy, you can see it in their eyes." Ella widened hers. "You won't notice it while you're drunk, but the pictures will be horrendous."

Jasmine flashed Katrina a *help me* look, but the succubus laughed. "Give me your phone, Ella. I'll take it for you." She made a grabby motion with her hand. "Quickly, before your eyes get drunk."

Ella handed her phone to the demon, and Jasmine

walked arm in arm with her to the party, standing next to her in the bride tribe line-up.

"Hold on." Raina untangled her arms from the bridesmaids on either side of her and faced the group. "Of course it's Jasmine in the wrong place. Ella is not the 'she' to your 'nanigans.' I am." Taking Jasmine's shoulders, she jerked her out of the lineup and placed her on the other side of the group.

Stepping back, Raina dusted her hands on her pants. Whether it was to wipe off the morgue remnants from touching her or to indicate she'd completed a job well done, Jasmine wasn't sure. She didn't take offense either way. She'd lost count of the number of times people wiped off their palms after shaking her hand.

No one wanted to touch a person who had their hands on dead bodies. Imagine how they'd feel if they knew what she could do with a body and a soul!

"There." Raina wedged herself back into the middle of the group. "Now all the arrows are pointing at me like they should be."

Katrina fought a grin and winked at Jasmine. "All right, ladies, on three I want you all to say 'three-way.' One. Two."

"Three-way," they all shouted in unison and then broke out into a fit of giggles.

As Jasmine slowly backed away from the increasingly inebriated party, a chill in the air raised goosebumps on her arms. The hairs on the back of her neck stood on end, and her skin tingled like she was covered in menthol muscle cream.

She whipped around in the direction the sensation was coming from, and her breath caught at the sight.

Ghosts normally appeared to her as real as humans.

She didn't have to activate her magic, ring any bells, or chant any spells to see them like a simple medium would. If the spirit was manifesting in the earthly realm, she could see it plain as day.

But ghosts always appeared in grayscale. It was like death sucked all the color out of you the moment you passed on. Anyone who'd seen a corpse after a day or two of decomposition would understand. Color was life, and without that living energy, everything turned gray.

Spirits were also transparent. The weaker the ghost, the more see-through they were, but this guy on the dance floor...this... Jasmine tilted her head. Was that a pirate? He was as solid as a living being, but he was also gray like a ghost.

Whether he was actually a spirit from another century or just a guy in body paint and regalia, she couldn't tell—it was New Orleans, after all—but he had long, curly black hair, and he wore a waistcoat with tails, tall boots, and a feathered pirate hat. He stood, rubbing his thumb and forefinger on his chin as he watched a guy grinding with a woman on the dance floor.

He had a curious expression, and when the man grabbed the woman by the butt, pressing his hips into hers, the pirate's eyebrows shot up. He took a long stride toward them, wiggling his hips with the music as if trying to mimic the other dancers.

"Do you see that guy?" Jasmine nudged Katrina on the arm. This had to be the first time she'd ever been unsure whether a person was living or dead. *How strange.*

"The tall one who's all up in that woman's business?" She licked her lips, her eyes flashing red briefly before returning to their usual shade of lavender. "I sure do, and he makes me wish I wasn't fasting."

"Not him. The guy behind them. The one dressed like a pirate."

"A pirate?" Katrina squinted as if she couldn't see well —which was ridiculous because demons had perfect eyesight, especially in the dark. "I don't see a pirate."

"Dammit." It didn't appear anyone else could see him either, which meant—regardless of his solid form—he had to be a ghost. "I've never seen one so strong."

"Is it a spirit? What's he doing?"

"I think he's trying to dance." Jasmine inched closer as the pirate moved up behind the woman and attempted to dance with her. She shivered, swatting the back of her neck and turning around in a circle. Her arm passed right through the pirate's form, but he didn't even flinch.

Yep, definitely a ghost. And strong enough that a human could sense him. The quizzical way he watched the people dancing, and the fact that he didn't react when she passed through him meant he'd been dead for a very long time.

Not good.

"How fun." Katrina's form shimmered, her soccer mom guise giving way for her true succubus form. "I wish I could see it."

The men standing closest to them locked their gazes on the succubus, their mouths falling slack. Who could blame them? Katrina was beautiful with her glamour on. Without it, she was a mashup between Aphrodite and the hottest stripper in New Orleans.

"I think your demon is starting to show." Jasmine jerked her head toward the men.

"Oh, poo." Katrina reined in her sexual magic, and the men blinked as if they'd forgotten what they were doing. "It's hard to keep my glamour up in a place like this.

Nearly everyone here is looking to get laid…and laying is my specialty."

"Well, I'm not, and neither are you. Consider me your anti-wingman."

"You're right." She smoothed her hair into her ponytail and straightened her spine. "I'll never be free from hell with that attitude."

"Let me see what's up with the ghost, and then we can leave." Jasmine put on her bubble of protection and weaved her way through the crowd toward the spirit. "Hey," she whispered into the air. The ghost would hear her no matter the volume of her voice, and with the bass thumping, none of the living would notice her over the noises of the club.

The moment her word hit the pirate, he froze and slowly turned toward her. Recognition flashed in his eyes —spirits always knew what she was—and he darted into the crowd.

"Oh, you wanna play hide and seek, do you?" Jasmine closed her eyes and put her feelers out into the room. The only ghost in the building, his energy was so strong it only took her a second to find him, and she latched onto him with her mind.

"Stop." She pulled him toward her and opened her eyes, a smug smile curving her lips. She'd never met a ghost strong enough to slip from her grasp, and this guy was *not* going to be the first.

The pirate looked at her, narrowing his eyes for a moment before a sinister smile crooked his ashy lips. He bowed formally, and with a wink, he ripped from her metaphysical grasp, absorbing into the aether like a broken tortilla chip disappearing into a bowl of queso.

"Holy cheese balls."

CHAPTER FOUR

The streets of the French Quarter would have looked normal to a human or even a supe without the ability to see the dead. But to Asher, the place was a nightmare. Ghosts floated in and out of buildings, congregating on sidewalks and rushing the living, laughing as people squealed and jumped, swatting at the air when their invisible assailants couldn't be found.

At a rate of nearly eight hundred deaths per week in Asher's jurisdiction, his little vacation meant sixteen hundred spirits who should have crossed over were now hanging out on Earth. And from the looks of it, they'd all come to New Orleans.

Some—the ones who behaved in life and had a decent afterlife waiting for them—probably came looking for him. Others—the ones who were afraid of what awaited them and those who didn't know they were dead—had simply been drawn here by his energy. Asher had lived topside in New Orleans for the past twenty-eight years, so his mark on this city was strong.

As he trudged up the street—racking his brain for a

solution to his problem—an erotic moan sounded from an alley, and a woman stumbled out, smiling as she rubbed her neck and joined her friends at a bar's to-go window.

"Must be nice to be a vampire," he mumbled. All vamps had to worry about was finding a secluded spot to have a meal. They weren't born with a single purpose like reapers. Hell, vampires weren't even born; they were made. And Asher's purpose…

He refused to accept he was *that* reaper. The one destined to lose his immortality to love. What was love, anyway? A fleeting human emotion that might grant him a few decades of happiness in exchange for giving up everything he'd ever known and everything he was meant to be. Until two weeks ago, he'd been a damn good reaper. One of the best. He'd screwed up royally, yes. But he was going to fix it.

He'd get his door unlocked, and then he'd move back to the aether where he belonged. Away from people. Away from Jasmine and the temptation to kiss eternity goodbye.

"Asher, my good friend." Gaston stepped out of the alley and bowed formally. With his pale skin and ice-blue eyes, the ancient vampire could almost pass for a reaper. His long dark hair, which he wore pulled back in a band, was the only feature that would give him away. Death had light hair.

"Hey, man." Asher nodded.

"I'd say you look as though you've been to hell and back, but given the fact you make that trip regularly, it doesn't properly describe your appearance." He draped an arm over his shoulders and guided him away from the alley. "You look like sweltering untidiness."

"You mean a hot mess? Because that's how I feel."

"It's nothing a little libation with an old comrade can't

solve, I'm sure. Join me on Bourbon Street? It's ladies' night at my favorite bar." Gaston wiggled his eyebrows in emphasis.

"Not even a slice of Sweet Destiny's heavenly devil's food cake can help me solve this problem, I'm afraid. I screwed up bad."

"How bad?"

Asher shoved his hands in his pockets. "All hell's breaking loose."

"I see. Well, it can't get much worse, can it? Let's have a drink and see if we can come up with a solution for your predicament."

"Might as well." Asher kept his gaze trained on the club entrance, doing his best to avoid looking directly at any of the spirits. The dead could see the living with no problem. Ninety-nine percent of the living couldn't sense the dead, so as long as they didn't figure out he could see them, they'd leave him be.

At least…they usually left him be.

"You!" A ghost with a massive bite taken out of his neck floated toward him. "I know you can see me. You looked right at me."

Satan's balls. He'd glanced briefly at the guy's gruesome injury, and now he was on him like stink on a ten-day-old corpse.

"Are you the reaper? Can you help us?"

Gaston stepped inside the club, but the ghost hovered in the entrance, blocking Asher's path. If he acknowledged the dead guy, he'd spread the word to the other spirits, and with sixteen hundred dead people knowing who Asher was and what he was supposed to do with them, he'd be in it so deep he'd never swim his way out. It was best not to let on that he could see them at all.

The only way out of this predicament was to go straight through it. Taking a deep breath and reeling in his magic, Asher ground his teeth and stepped through the spirit. With his powers intact, he'd have felt the ghost as a solid form, much like a living being, though colder and harder. To pass through it, he had to wad his reaper magic into a little ball, holding it tight inside his core, making his body as human on the inside as it currently looked on the outside.

In this warm, flesh and blood state, a feeling of jagged ice dragged through his insides as he passed the spirit's space and entered the club. He tried not to react, but he couldn't avoid the involuntary shudder as the cold dissipated from his system. Not daring to turn around to see if the spirit followed, he headed straight for the bar where Gaston stood waiting for him.

He ordered a beer and had barely pressed the bottle to his lips when the necromancer's energy plowed into him.

"What have you done?" Jasmine Lee marched toward him wearing a hot pink bachelorette party t-shirt with zebra print writing and not looking at all happy about it. She scowled at Gaston, keeping her distance from the vampire as she directed her anger toward Asher. "This is a disaster."

You have no idea. His chest tightened the moment her dark eyes locked with his, a hollow achiness expanding in his heart, reminding him why he'd felt the need to run in the first place. So. Many. Emotions…

He took a swig of his beer, stalling so he could compose himself. The icy bubbles tickled on their way down his throat, and he let his gaze meander over Jasmine's outfit. "Don't blame me for your friend's taste in clothing. Animal print belongs on animals."

The collar of the shirt she'd originally worn peeked out from the neck of the bachelorette getup, which meant she hadn't planned the ensemble herself, but her black pants did accent the stripes nicely. Her long, raven hair cascaded over her shoulders, and though her pink lips turned downward in a frown, he couldn't help but linger his gaze a little too long.

This woman could be the literal death of him...the death of *Death*. He should've bid her *beep beep* and taken off like the Roadrunner fleeing from Wile E. Coyote, yet all he could think about was taking her in his arms and making her his for the rest of their brief mortal lives. *Get it together, reaper.*

"I think you look quite lovely, Miss Jasmine." Gaston stepped toward her, and she threw up a hand.

"Back off, vampire, or I'll do your soul a favor and rip it from that rotting corpse."

Gaston straightened, a slow smile bowing his lips. "I assure you, this body is far from rotting. Allow me to escort you home, and you'll find it quite lively."

"Dude." Asher nudged Gaston back toward the bar, shaking his head. "Sorry about...him," he said to Jasmine. The way Gaston was looking at her, running his tongue over his teeth...his fangs fully extended...the spark of jealousy burning in Asher's chest turned to alarm. He spent plenty of time around vampires, and he'd never seen one react that way.

Jasmine shrugged one shoulder. "Vampires are drawn to necromancers. It's nothing new." She waved off his apology. "You, on the other hand, have been ignoring my calls. Where have you been?"

"You called me?" His stomach fluttered at the idea. "My phone died. I..." He raked a hand through his hair.

Seriously, man. Get it together. "I'm here now. How can I be of service?"

She crossed her arms. "You can unlock your door to the underworld and send the mess of ghosts that ambushed me through. I don't have time to babysit a bunch of spirits."

He opened his mouth to respond, but what could he say? He couldn't tell her the truth: that he had no idea how to open it unless he could find the ghost that used his entrance as an exit. She already hated him for the way he'd treated her. If she knew how badly he screwed up, she'd think he was incompetent too.

"There's um…" He glanced at Gaston for help, but his vampire friend pushed from the bar, his gazed locked on a tall brunette on her way toward the exit. "There's been a glitch with the doors to hell. I'm sure it'll be fixed soon."

He clamped his mouth shut, keeping his expression neutral. Even he wanted to roll his eyes at the lame excuse, but he couldn't stand for her to think any worse of him.

"A glitch?" She blinked, unconvinced. "Since when does hell glitch?"

"Not hell itself." He gulped down his beer, hoping the liquid courage would help him dig his way out of this mess. "Just the…doors?"

"The doors to hell are glitching, and they're locked?"

He nodded slowly.

Her jaw ticked. "And the lights are out?"

"Mm-hmm?" Was she buying this or not? He couldn't tell.

Pursing her lips, she glanced at the ceiling as if mulling over his excuse. "That makes sense. The ghosts I talked to said your door was locked. Some of them couldn't even find the light."

"Yep, that's the glitch. The doors to the underworld have a soft glow that humans call "the light." When they lock, the light goes out. The guys in hell aren't sure what happened, but I'm working on fixing it." He swallowed hard. Technically, he wasn't lying. The door being locked was the equivalent of a glitch, and if anyone in hell knew what had happened, they'd have sent word to him by now. Then again, if anyone had tried to call…

"Are you okay?" For the first time since he'd hurt her, she looked at him with an expression other than disdain. "You seem grimmer than usual."

"Grimmer. That's funny." He couldn't help but laugh at her pun. She always knew how to make him smile. Until he screwed it all up. "Yeah, I'm fine. Just… If you can turn off your ability…shut out the ghosts for a while, you might want to do that. Can you do that?"

She scoffed. "I'm the most powerful necromancer in New Orleans. I could put them all in a conga line and make them do the limbo if I wanted to."

His eyes widened as an idea formed in his mind. "You could gather them up, put them in a line for questioning?"

"I could make them do the hokey pokey. What's your point?"

He shouldn't be asking this of her. She was the one person he needed to stay away from, but she might be the only one who could help him. "My phone is my only way to communicate with my superiors in hell, and with it dead—"

"I didn't realize the underworld relied so much on human technology." She arched a brow. "You're like two hundred years old. How'd you stay in touch before phones?"

"It just looks like a phone to blend in. Well, it works

like a phone too, but that's not the point. We've always used some kind of magical call box. Mine used to look like a pocket watch."

"Did it tell time?"

"Of course. And without it, I don't know which spirits are due in the underworld and which are supposed to roam the Earth for a while." Nor did he know which one of the little bastards had already been in hell and escaped. "With my door locked, I can't get into hell to get the information or a new phone."

"Sounds like you need to find another way into hell. I can't help you with that."

"Hey, Jasmine." Katrina glided toward them, resting a hand on her shoulder. "Flirting with Death, I see." Her gaze raked up and down Asher's body, and he could almost feel the sexual energy radiating from her. "Are you going to get a room? Can I watch?"

Asher, being from the underworld himself, could usually tell what kind of magic a demon possessed, even though they rarely revealed their true powers. But Katrina sucked at hiding her succubus nature. She was a demon, though, and he did need a ticket to hell. Maybe he could do this without Jasmine's help.

"You can if you'll do me a favor."

Jasmine shook her head. "This is as close to a near-Death experience as I'll ever have. Let's go, Kat."

Katrina smirked, linking her arm around Jasmine's elbow. "Just a minute. I'm not in the business of doing favors, but I'd like to hear what this delicious specimen of a man needs. Perhaps you could service him…"

"Ew." Jasmine wrinkled her nose.

Asher tried to ignore the sting. *Service* wasn't the best

word to describe what the succubus implied, but was the thought of being with him really that off-putting to her now? Had he ruined any chance he might have with her? If so, was that a good thing or a bad thing? *Focus on the issue, man.* "My door to hell is locked. Can you give me a lift?"

Katrina blinked, her confidence slipping to show her true vulnerability. "And that's my cue to leave. I'm not sorry, Asher. I will never return to that place. Ever. Shall we?" She motioned with her head toward the party, and Jasmine turned to leave with her.

"Jasmine…" He took her hand, and confusion flashed in her eyes before she tugged from his grasp.

"I'll be right there, Kat." Her gaze bounced from his eyes to his lips, the hollow ache in his chest expanding with her hesitation.

The strange expression on her face disarmed him, and he stumbled over his words. "Maybe…maybe you could gather up the ghosts while I…"

"Are you serious?" Her composure regained, she fisted her hands on her hips. "After I… And then you… You've taken spirits you knew I needed to the underworld, making my job ten times harder, when you could have left them for a day and let me do my thing. Not to mention…" She clamped her mouth shut.

No, *that* didn't need mentioning. "I was just doing my job."

"Yeah, well, so was I, but you made it impossible. I almost *lost* my job because of you."

"I was following the rules."

"Which are apparently more important than people. Than *friends*. Rules can be bent. Hell, sometimes they should be broken."

"I can't..." He *did*. He did break the rules, and look what happened.

"I know you can't, Asher. You were 'born' to reap souls. You've made your excuses, and I'm not buying them. No, I won't help you. I think you can manage fifteen lost souls." She spun on her heel, flipping her hair over her shoulder and wafting the sweet scent of honeysuckle shampoo into the air.

Fifteen lost souls? If that's how small she thought this problem was, she was in for a big surprise the moment she left the club.

CHAPTER FIVE

"That was not cool, Katrina." Jasmine glanced over her shoulder as she walked away, but Asher was already sulking toward the exit. *Good. Let him sulk.*

"If you'd been to hell, you'd understand why I refuse to go back, even for a second."

"Oh, I don't blame you for that. I don't want to help him either. I'm talking about you turning on your succubus magic while I was talking to my arch nemesis. All I could think about was grabbing on to him and finding out if Death tastes as sinful as it looks."

Katrina snickered.

"It's not funny. I've had dozens of arguments with Asher in my head, so I have plenty of ammunition. So many witty comebacks, but noooo. My succubus best friend decided to scramble my brain with hormones. So, yeah. Thanks for that."

Her snicker grew into a full-on laugh. "Oh, honey. I did nothing but bask in the sexual attraction that already exists between you two. Any *hormones* or naughty thoughts you had came from *you*."

"I..." Jasmine's jaw worked, but her brain couldn't seem to form words. She didn't still have feelings for him. Sure, the reaper was hot as sin, but he was her enemy. A soul thief. A stickler for the rules, and when you're dealing with death, you have to play it by ear.

All he cared about was his job, so why should she help him? He certainly didn't care about her. He'd made that clear as a freshly cleaned window when he ghosted her. Then again, she'd never seen him quite so helpless-looking. Her stomach sank. Maybe she should have...

"What did you do to the poor guy?" Ella met her at the edge of the dance floor. "He nearly gave me a panic attack, with all the worry rolling off him. Why didn't you take him home and make him forget his troubles? You obviously wanted to."

Jasmine reeled on her sister. "First of all, why were you prodding into our emotions? We had a deal. I don't point out every ghost I see, and you keep your bubble on and mind your own business."

Ella threw an arm over Jasmine's shoulders, causing them both to stumble as she absorbed her sister's weight. "You know it's hard to keep my ability in check when I drink, and those hurricanes are too good to pass up. They go down like liquid candy." She giggled and kissed Jasmine on the cheek. "What's second?"

"Second." She unwound Ella's arm and held on until she was steady. "You know I hate Asher, and even if I didn't, he's a reaper. They aren't capable of normal human emotions."

"Asher's different," Katrina said. "He does live topside, so maybe..."

Jasmine used to think he was different too, but he proved her wrong. "I still hate him."

"There's a fine line between love and hate, sis, and you are standing clearly on the L-word side."

Jasmine scoffed. "Not even close."

"You know, you don't have to like each other to have amazing sex." Katrina winked at Ella before flashing a devilish grin at Jasmine. "Hate is a passionate emotion. Sometimes it's better when—"

Jasmine held up her hands. "Stop it. Both of you. I'm not going to sleep with Asher, so just get over yourselves. He's not interested." And neither was she. Not anymore.

"Oh, he's interested," Ella said. "I need to be around y'all when I'm sober to sort it all out, though. The man is full of emotion—the *human* kind—and, aside from the near-panic, most of it is directed at you."

"I guarantee you, it's not. I don't like Asher, and he has made it abundantly clear he's not into me, so drop it, okay?"

Ella narrowed her eyes. "There's something you're not telling us."

Jasmine lifted her hands, flustered. "I hate him. That's it."

"Yeah, but that hate is sitting on a solid foundation of a whole mess of other emotions I'm too tipsy to sort through, so spill it, sister. What's the real story with you and the reaper?"

Katrina clasped her hands beneath her chin. "Yes, Jasmine, do tell."

Jasmine closed her eyes for a long blink, her nostrils flaring as she let out a slow breath. Her cheeks burned, and while she'd rather turn around and march her ass right out of the club, these two wouldn't let up until she spilled the tea. "You wanna know the real story? Fine. I know

Asher isn't interested because I kissed him once, and he didn't kiss me back."

"That bastard." Ella crossed her arms. "What happened?"

"He used to be nice to me. We were actually friends for a while." She laughed, but there wasn't any humor in it. "Unfortunately, I didn't inherit a lick of the empathic ability you have, and the romantic attraction I thought was growing between us turned out to be one-sided." She slid onto a stool and rested her elbow on the table. "This is why I don't get out much."

"Go on," Katrina urged.

"We were at Trace and Sophie's wedding, having a great time, so I told him I liked him and I thought we'd be good together." He'd been flirting with her. Hell, he'd done the classic tuck her hair behind her ear move, so he had to be. Love was in the air, though, and she might have gotten ahead of herself, but c'mon… a reaper and a necromancer? Two friends with somewhat similar abilities falling in love after a sweet friendship… how perfect would that be?

"Then I leaned in and planted one on him. He froze, so I stopped and apologized. He mumbled something and started looking at the door, so I asked him point-blank. 'It's the corpse thing, isn't it?' Because that's the problem everyone else has with me, you know? And he said, 'Corpses are…' Then his phone pinged; he said he had to go, and rather than walking out the door, he ripped a hole in the air and disappeared." He wanted to get away from her so fast, he didn't even take the time to walk. How sad was that?

"The conversation you witnessed tonight is the longest one I've had with him since…" Since he'd broken her heart. She shrugged, the weight of her shoulders making her posture sag.

"Oh, Jazz." Ella squeezed her hand.

"How pathetic is it that even a *reaper* thinks I'm disgusting?" Her eyes started to water, so she blinked, trying to get the dust out. It was dust, or maybe it was chemicals from the fog machine. Did the club use a fog machine? Whatever it was, she had to make it stop before her sister and her best friend assumed she was getting weepy over the guy.

She was *so* not getting weepy.

"He does not think you're disgusting. Where is he?" Her sister spun toward the bar. "I'm going to march my perturbed butt up to that reaper and give him a piece of my mind. While I'm at it, I'll unleash the full power of my empathic ability and find out *exactly* how he feels about you."

"No, Ella." Jasmine clutched her sister's arm. "Don't. He's gone, anyway." And she didn't want to know how he really felt. She knew how he'd made *her* feel, and that was enough. She didn't really hate Asher. He was the embodiment of Death, after all. But it was easier to direct her anger at him than to admit she'd fallen for a being incapable of love.

Katrina twirled a lock of hair around her finger. "I can make him go limp for a while, if that will make you feel better. It's temporary, but that's one aspect of my magic I don't mind using."

Jasmine stood and put a hand on each of their shoulders. "While I'm sure your hearts are in the right place, that really won't be necessary. It's never going to happen between me and Asher, okay? I'm just going to file it away with the corpses at the morgue because this topic is dead."

"The best way to get over a man is to get *under* someone else." Katrina swept her gaze across the crowd. "Let me find you a hottie to hook up with."

"No." Jasmine shook her head. "I'm fine. Really."

Katrina pouted her lower lip. "You're no fun at all. I was hoping to live vicariously through you, but I can see I need to find another friend to set up."

"I'm game." Ella wiggled her eyebrows.

Jasmine groaned. "Have I been here long enough to appease Bridezilla? The last thing I need is Aunt Patricia calling Mom to complain about my behavior…again."

Ella looked over her shoulder where Raina was doing shots with two bridesmaids. "I think you're fine. I doubt she's going to remember much about tonight."

"Hallelujah." Jasmine tugged at the party shirt, but her sister shook her head.

"That's yours to keep. Call me tomorrow."

"Gee, thanks. You coming, Katrina?"

"I think I'll stick around a while and see if I can't find a date for your twin. At least one of you needs to get laid tonight."

Jasmine chuckled. "Y'all have fun."

She slowly made her way toward the exit, taking her time to avoid running into Asher on the street. Standing close to the man for ten minutes had unearthed all the painful emotions she'd been trying to bury, and if Katrina was telling the truth—that she had nothing to do with the weak-in-the-knees, fluttery-stomach feelings Jasmine had for Asher—she needed to keep her distance before he shredded her heart all over again.

As she stepped through the exit, Cameron's ghostly energy latched on to her, pulling the warmth from her body. Dammit, she'd let her guard slip after that weird encounter with the pirate and the even weirder way Asher had made her feel.

She threw up her shields and used her power to push the spirit out of her personal space. "What did I tell you about getting too close?"

"Sorry. Was that him? The blond guy? He looked right at me. Was he the reaper? Can he help?"

"Yeah, about that. He said there's a glitch or something, and that's why the door is locked. He's working on it, so just hang tight. I'm sure it'll be fixed soon."

Cameron's brow furrowed. "I can do that, but what about all of them?"

He thumbed over his shoulder, and Jasmine lifted her gaze to the street behind him. *Holy phantom farts.* There had to be a hundred ghosts on Bourbon Street, and they were all looking at her.

"Maybe I should have helped Asher."

CHAPTER SIX

A sher shoved the last bite of devil's food cake into his mouth and closed his eyes, letting the rich, decadent chocolate soothe his frazzled nerves. After his failed attempt at getting Katrina's or Jasmine's help last night— not that he'd expected them to agree, especially not Jasmine—he'd taken the rest of the night to mull over the issue and attempt to sleep.

Well, he tried to sleep after he roamed the French Quarter for a few hours, making sure the ghosts weren't causing more trouble than the *Vieux Carré* was used to. So far, the spirits seemed complacent…even confused as to why they were in New Orleans and not moving on to the underworld. He had time, but not much, and getting back into hell was the only way to fix this.

After scraping the last bit of frosting from his plate, he licked it off the fork and stood. The pink wrought iron chair scraped across the wooden floor, and Destiny, the Earth-bound angel who owned the bakery, appeared from the kitchen.

"And? Did the chocolate ease your woes?"

He rolled his neck from side to side, and sure enough, some of the tension in his muscles had eased. "I don't know what kind of magic you bake into that cake, but it's heavenly."

"It's just a smidge of cannabis. The THC calms the nerves."

He cocked his head. "You're serving pot-laced desserts? Is that how you subdue the demons too?"

She laughed. "I'm kidding. There's no magic in devil's food cake, aside from the power of chocolate."

"Chocolate makes everything better."

"As for the demons, that's a top-secret, highly addictive bit of magic very few of us are licensed to use. An overdose could strip a demon of its power, throwing off the magical balance of the city, and who knows what would happen then."

Part of Destiny's job here on Earth was to keep the demons who called New Orleans home in check. She did so by serving them angel food cakes infused with magic that subdued their demonic power, helping them suppress the urges that would otherwise wreak havoc on the city.

He toyed with the scythe-turned-pen in his pocket. "Do you have a reverse version of that magic? Something to increase power?"

Sympathy softened her eyes as she pressed her lips together. "I thought I sensed more than your usual frustration about being overworked. I'm afraid I can't help you with your magic, but I'm a good listener. Maybe I can help you find a solution?"

"Thanks, but I know what I have to do." Hopefully he wouldn't be thrown in the tarpits when he did it.

Exiting the bakery, he made a left on Magazine Street and headed for the establishment next door. Honoré's, an authentic, demon-run Cajun restaurant, was housed in a blue nineteenth-century Victorian mansion with white gingerbread trim and an expansive front porch. Two massive oak trees towered on either side of the walk, their shade providing a welcome relief from the sweltering summer heat.

His shoes thudded on the original hardwood floor as he entered and weaved his way through the tables toward the back of the restaurant, and he caught a glimpse of himself in the mirror behind the bar. Even after two weeks on the beach, he was paler than a vampire's ass.

"Asher, how was the vacation?" Mike, a half-human Devil's Advocate, offered his hand to shake. He was a recovering demon—meaning he'd won his freedom and no longer had to make deals on Satan's behalf—but Asher still hesitated to accept the gesture. Old habits and all.

Mike chuckled. "My palm isn't burning, so I know I'm not offering a deal."

"Not even accidentally?"

"How about a hug instead?" Mike opened his arms. "I missed you, man."

Asher gave his friend a quick hug, patting him on the back before stepping away. "I need a favor."

"You know I'm not in the business anymore."

"Not a deal. A favor between friends." He raked a hand through his hair. "I screwed up, and I need your help to fix it."

Mike's smile faded, his brow furrowing over dark eyes. "Sounds serious. Come on back."

Asher followed the demon into an office and closed the door. Mike would hate him for asking this. There was a chance he might not even do it, but he had to try.

"What's going on?" Mike leaned on the edge of a desk and gestured toward a chair for Asher to sit.

He paced the length of the small room instead, recounting the story of his epic screw-up and everything that had happened since he decided to take some time off.

Mike blinked. "A thousand ghosts?"

"More. They're swarming the French Quarter. So far, they aren't causing too much trouble. People are used to hauntings in New Orleans. Hell, it might even help tourism for a while, but I'll have to escort them all to the underworld eventually."

"How are you going to figure out which one of them is the escapee?"

"With my phone on the fritz and no way to contact Charon, I need to find a way into hell."

Wariness furrowed Mike's brow. "Can't you portal there?"

"Reapers can't portal directly into the underworld. If we were dropping souls off willy nilly all over the place, it would be impossible to process them. We each have our own magical door just outside the border, and it's the only way we can get in." He clenched his fists. "I can portal to the door, but I'm locked out of hell."

Mike paused, Asher's unasked question hanging between them. He nodded slowly as he pushed from the desk and strolled around to the chair behind it. "Can you use another reaper's door? Do you need help locating one?"

"No."

"That's what I thought." Mike sank into the chair, resting his elbows on the desk and shoving his fingers into his dark hair.

"Reapers follow a strict code of conduct, and we..."

Asher's jaw ticked. "*They* never break the rules. There's literally no way in hell another reaper would give me access to his door, especially after someone escaped through mine."

Mike stood. "I'm guessing you need me to open a portal that doesn't require a door for you? Get you down to hell the demon way?"

Asher's eyes tightened. "Remember how I risked my ass to take Crimson down to find you, loaded her on the ferry and delivered her to Satan's palace even though she'd been struck from the list?"

Mike smiled, but it didn't reach his eyes. "I'm happy to open a portal for you. It's the least I can do."

"I need you to go with me. Without you, I'd have to leave through my own door too, and it'll be locked until I find the ghost that escaped, so…" He gave Mike his most apologetic look.

"You want me to go back to hell with you?" Mike's expression was incredulous. "I've only been free a few months."

"I know. Believe me, I've racked my brain for another solution, but this is all I can come up with. I need to talk to Charon, figure out who escaped so I can find him and send his soul back to the underworld where it belongs before New Orleans becomes a literal hell on Earth. Will you help me?"

Mike took a deep breath, nodding once. "I'd be making deals with the miscreants in Los Angeles, never to see the love of my life again, if it weren't for you. Of course I'll take you." He took a white pastry box from the mini fridge behind the desk. "I keep a stash of Destiny's angel food cake back here for emergencies. Hopefully it'll be enough to keep my powers in check while we're down there."

Mike shoved a miniature cake into his mouth. "Damn, these are good. One more, and I'll be good to go. I hope." He ate one more piece and returned the box to the fridge. "You ready?"

"As I'll ever be."

This time, when Mike offered his hand, Asher took it. With a wave of his other arm, the demon tore a hole through reality, and they stepped into hell. As the portal closed, a blood-curdling scream sliced through the stagnant air, followed by a warbled-sounding howl.

"Satan really needs to update his welcome music." Mike gestured to a worn stone path leading out of the demon entrance to the underworld. "How long ago did you buy that soundtrack?"

"I think it was ninety-four. I'm surprised the tape player still works."

"Well, this is hell."

"True." Asher breathed in the sulfurous smell of the underworld. Hot and humid, the air didn't feel much different than New Orleans in July, but he'd take the sweet aromas of magnolias and beignets over this poisonous stench any day.

They made their way through hell, past the winding, two-mile-long line for general soul processing before stopping at the edge of the River Styx. Across the raging rapids, Asher glimpsed The Rock. Every reaper's door opened onto the massive boulder positioned in the middle of the river, though his was the only one he could see.

Charon docked at the edge of the precipice, his ferry magically extending to accommodate the group of souls boarding it. The ancient entity locked his gaze on Asher, and though he was clear across the river, the scowl on his face was unmistakable. *Oh, shit.*

Mike peered over the rocky bank into the boiling obsidian water below. "Have you ever lost a soul in there? Rumor has it they'll be boiled alive for all eternity if they fall in."

"Yet you're standing right on the edge. It's probably true for half-humans too."

Mike took a giant step backward. "Good point."

"I've seen two fall in over the two hundred-ish years I've been doing this." He shrugged. "I warned them not to get too close to the edge, but you know how humans can be. Telling them 'no' makes them want to do it even more."

"Here comes your boss." Mike backed up even more as Charon docked his ferry, the boat shrinking to the size of a gondola as the last soul exited onto the shore.

While the humans shuffled toward the processing line, Charon rose to his full seven-foot height and stepped off the boat, his black robes dragging the ground as he stalked toward Asher.

"Where in the Devil's name have you been?" Charon's eye twitched in its deep-set socket as he growled through clenched teeth.

"I, uh…" Asher's voice cracked, so he cleared his throat. "I took a vacation."

"Reapers don't go on vacation, you imbecile!" Clutching Asher's shirt, Charon lifted him from the ground and hurled him into the River Styx.

Boiling water engulfed him, and though he was immortal, it hurt like hell. The raging current dragged him away from the dock, and he closed his eyes against the stinging, acidic water, digging in his pocket for his pen.

Holy hellhounds, this was pure torture. It felt like his skin was melting off the bone. He hadn't thought twice about the two souls who'd fallen in years ago, but now he'd have to petition Satan to fish them out and send them on their way. Of course, he'd have to solve his own problems first. Where the hell was his pen?

His fingers wrapped around the plastic, and he yanked it from his pocket. With a click of the depressor, it transformed into his trusty scythe, and he tore open a portal to the shore. A wave of boiling water crashed through with him, the liquid turning to steam as it splattered on the stones around his feet.

Charon picked at his nails like he didn't have a care in the world. "Took you long enough to get back. Your power is diminishing with your door locked."

Mike cringed, shuddering like he'd experienced the river himself. "Are you okay?"

Asher ran a hand through his soaking wet hair—at least it had cooled to room temperature—and wrung the water from his shirt. "I've been better." He glared at Charon. "Was that really necessary?"

"I've been trying to reach you for a week and a half, and you were on *vacation?* You haven't delivered a soul in two weeks, and one of your inmates has escaped through your door." His hollow eyes flashed red flames. "Not only was it necessary, but you should have stayed in longer."

Charon shoved Asher again, but this time he was ready. His scythe already extended, he sliced a hole in the air before his face met the rapids. He may have avoided the boiling river, but as he fell out of the portal, he face-planted on the shore instead.

Solid rock smashing into the nose didn't feel good, even to immortals, and his eyes watered as he rose to his feet and moved next to Mike, who rightly had moved six feet back from the water's edge.

"Yes, I screwed up. I turned off my phone, and when it powered back on, I had so many souls on my list, they fried it. I need a new one."

Charon snatched the phone from his hand. "*I* need a new reaper. I should fire you and exile you to the tarpits for this."

"Why don't you?" Mike asked matter-of-factly.

"Seriously?" Asher scoffed. "I thought we were friends."

"I'm not saying he should." Mike held up his hands. "But if he were going to, he'd have done it by now, so there must be something else going on. In fact, a guard should have come along and grabbed you the moment you stepped into hell." He looked at Charon. "Why haven't you reported him to Satan?"

Charon inclined his chin. "Because I'm his supervisor. I'm responsible for all the reapers, and his mistake makes me look bad."

"Is that all?" Mike prodded.

Charon huffed. "The escaped soul stowed away on my ferry to make it to The Rock in the first place. Asher left his door unattended, but it was I who *unknowingly* provided the escape vehicle."

Mike laughed. "Yeah, I don't think the big guy's going to care about the *unknowingly* part."

Charon crossed his arms, his long bony fingers drumming against his robe. "So you see my dilemma."

Asher's head spun. Mike was right. He *should* have been apprehended the moment he stepped into hell, but he'd been so focused on finding Charon, he hadn't even considered it. His mind was in too many places, thoughts of Jasmine scattering his senses like billiard balls every time he pictured her face. "I can fix this."

"You barely made it out of the water, and the longer your door remains locked, the weaker you'll become."

"All the more reason to find the bastard who escaped. We need to do a roll call. We'll make it sound routine…a centurial check to make sure everyone is where they're supposed to be."

"Oh, I know who escaped." Charon dropped Asher's phone into the depths of his robe and magically pulled out a new one. "Did you think I was sitting idly by as the list of missing souls increased by the day? You're lucky general processing is so backed up. When Satan is ready to begin the torment of the wicked ones, and he discovers they aren't here, he'll have both our heads on a platter."

"I hear since he dumped the banshee, he's back to collecting testicles." Mike shoved his hands into his pockets. "Maybe he'll just take one from each of you?"

Asher grimaced. "Not helpful, man."

Charon tapped the phone screen and offered it to Asher. "Your list is here, and everything is working properly. Do not turn it off again."

Asher shoved the phone into his back pocket. "Who am I looking for?"

Charon let out a sardonic laugh. "Do you remember a particularly ornery pirate from about two hundred years ago? I believe you had quite the time capturing him then. Imagine how strong he is now."

Asher's stomach sank. If Charon was talking about who he thought he was talking about, luck was most definitely *not* on his side. Even as a new spirit, the pirate had been slippery as a gator covered in vegetable shortening. Apparently, the ghost had done enough evil deeds in life that he knew what awaited him in the underworld, and he flat out refused to cooperate. It had taken Asher weeks to wrangle the specter through the door, and he'd had to go full-on reaper mode, skulking around in his skeletal form and wielding his scythe like a maniac to do it.

"So, there's a super-strong, nineteenth-century ghost pirate running around the French Quarter?" Mike laughed. "That's not even weird, considering the location."

Asher tapped his scythe, shrinking it into pen form. "You're not, by chance, talking about any pirate other than…"

"He's escaped, and you *will* find him, or I'll throw you into the tarpits myself." Charon folded his arms, his spindly hands disappearing into the billowing sleeves of his robe. "No one else from the underworld will know of this. Is that clear?" He looked from Asher to Mike.

Mike rubbed his palm on his jeans as a look of worry formed in his eyes. "I can probably work out a deal for you if—" He clamped his mouth shut, his nostrils flaring as he took a deep breath. "We need to go."

"No worries, Mike. I don't want to make a deal. I'll find the bastard."

"Satan cannot know of this," Charon said.

"I'm not planning to tell him, but if we don't get out of here soon, I can't make any guarantees." Mike jerked his head toward the demons' exit. "Being down here is bringing out the fiend in me."

"Thanks for the info." Asher clapped Charon on the shoulder. "I'll take care of it. I promise."

"You had better. We have far too few reapers as it is. I'd hate to banish you to an eternity of punishment when you could help us instead."

Asher followed Mike up the rocky path, grumbling as

he mulled over his predicament. His swim through the River Styx had drained him, making him feel achy and way more tired than he should. If his power was weakening this fast, he wouldn't have much time to find the ornery pirate before his door remained locked forever.

Mike had a pained look on his face. No doubt being in hell had activated his demonic urges, and he'd be itching to make a deal. What would Satan want in exchange for nabbing the errant soul and unlocking the door?

No. He couldn't even entertain the idea. The Devil always got the better end of the bargain, and Mike had just won his freedom. Asher would never ask him to go back to his old ways.

"Thanks for coming with me." Asher stopped next to his friend. "I know what it must be doing to you to be down here, and I appreciate the sacrifice."

"I'm glad to help. Who's the pirate you're looking for? Anyone famous?" Mike lifted his hand, his eyes glowing red as he opened a portal to Earth.

Asher shook his head, grinding his teeth. "It's Jean Lafitte."

The gateway glowed red around the edges, and Mike's office sat empty on the other side. He paused, turning his back to the opening and arching a brow in disbelief. "*The* Jean Lafitte? The Pirate King, The Terror of the Gulf?"

"The one and only."

CHAPTER SEVEN

Jasmine squeezed her eyes shut, trying her damnedest to ignore the incessant knocking coming from her front door. Her protective bubble only helped so much, and after trudging through a French Quarter overrun with the dead, her metaphysical battery was drained. She could've used a jumpstart, but borrowing energy from another person wasn't in her wheelhouse. Instead, she had to settle for a long night's sleep to recharge.

The knocking grew quieter, which meant the person trying to get her attention was running out of steam, which meant said person was also most likely dead. She groaned and rolled over, squinting blearily at the clock on her nightstand.

Eleven a.m. What was a ghost doing out near midday? Sure, spirits could manifest any time of day, but like most supernatural beings, their power increased with moonlight.

The doorknob rattled, and the spirit outside yelped, "Ouch!"

Despite her annoyance with the disturbance, the corners of her mouth tugged into a smile. Her magic-amplifying security perimeter worked like a charm.

"Jasmine?"

She recognized the gravelly voice and pulled a pillow over her head. Cameron could take a lesson in leaving her the hell alone from Asher.

Asher... *Oh, crap. All those ghosts.*

She slid out of bed and padded into the living room. A six-inch ball of wadded-up aluminum foil sat next to the door, and she rested a finger on it, waiting for the familiar buzz of her own amplified energy to register on her skin. Her hand tingled, so she rose and opened the door.

Sure enough, Cameron stood on the sidewalk outside. As he drifted toward her, he hit the invisible magic perimeter and jerked back, rubbing his arms and scowling after the shock he received. "Your house is electrified."

Jasmine leaned in the doorjamb. "It's magic to keep out the dead. A girl's gotta sleep."

"Have you heard from your reaper friend yet? It's getting bad out here."

She rolled her eyes at the way his voice held an edge of panic. The newly dead were so dramatic.

"First of all, I'd sooner befriend a rabid alligator with a severe case of flatulence than be friends with Asher." *That's right, girl. Keep telling yourself that.* "And, second, what do you mean bad? It's the middle of the day. It can't be any worse than last night."

"Have a look." Cameron floated back and gestured toward the street.

"Good gravy. What the hell is going on out there?"

Pure pandemonium, that was what. Ghosts were running, floating, flying up and down the streets like a fox had penetrated their chicken coop. Some were throwing punches—which actually registered because they were solid to each other—while others wrestled and some just screamed. It was like a kindergarten classroom on a sugar high after a Halloween party.

If that reaper didn't get his door unlocked soon, Jasmine wouldn't be able to step outside her apartment. She had no choice but to help him.

Cameron floated toward her, stopping short before her forcefield could shock him. "There's a pirate-looking guy who's sucking out the other spirits' energy. I think he was a vampire in life. Are vampires real?"

Jasmine groaned. "I think I know who you're talking about. He's not the blood-sucking kind of vampire, but sometimes really strong spirits can siphon energy from others." Like Cameron would be doing to her now if not for her magical barrier blocking him out. "He's an energy vampire, and he'll only get stronger."

"He's teaching the others how to do it. You have to save me from them. I'll do anything you want. I'll talk to the reaper for you if that will help, just please… Don't leave me out here alone with them."

Cameron's jaw trembled, and if ghosts could cry tears, they'd have been welling in the poor guy's eyes. She'd always had a soft spot for men who weren't afraid to show their emotions, and Cameron's raw vulnerability tugged at her heartstrings.

"How do you feel about fur?"

"What?" His shoulders slumped.

Jasmine picked up the aluminum ball, breaking the magical barrier, and jerked her head toward the living room. "Come in quick. I think I can keep you safe until this mess is figured out."

The ghost stepped into her home, and she replaced the ball, reactivating the shield around her space. "Keep your distance until I'm ready for you. That thing the pirate is doing to the others? You do it to me every time you get too close." She marched into the kitchen but paused. "Don't tell anyone about my weakness, okay? No one's supposed to know."

"My lips are sealed."

"Good." She opened the pantry and took out a can of tuna, popping the top and dumping it onto a paper plate. Cracking the back door open, she set the plate of fish on the patio next to the threshold. Then she retrieved a brown jar about the size of a funeral urn from another cabinet and set it on the counter. "This is an ouanga. I got it from a bokor out in the swamp."

"A bokor?" He eyed the container warily. "What's it for?"

"A bokor is a Voodoo practitioner who dances on the dark side of magic. Believe me, you do not want to cross one of these guys. *Holy wickedness.*" She shivered. "An ouanga is a jar that's been magically charged to hold souls."

Cameron jerked backward. "You're going to put me in a jar? That's not okay."

"I'm not going to put you in a jar." Movement in the corner of her eye drew her attention to the back door, where the cantankerous orange tomcat who liked to screech all day and spray his scent on her flower pots sat scarfing down the treat she'd laid out for him. "I'm going to put you in a cat."

"You're what?"

"Here, kitty, kitty," she whispered as she tip-toed toward the stray and grabbed him behind the shoulders.

The cat shrieked as she whisked him inside, hissing like a vampire with PMS.

She set him on the counter, reached inside his core with her mind, and gently plucked the consciousness from the feline, placing his grouchy personality in the ouanga. With his spiritual essence in the jar, the animal relaxed and curled into a ball on the granite, purring contentedly.

Cameron's mouth hung open as he cut his gaze between the jar and the cat. "I'm confused. If you just put the cat's soul into the jar, how is it still alive?" He floated closer to her, and a chill crept into her skin.

"Stand back or you'll go in the jar too, buddy." She rubbed her arms and shivered. "There are two parts to the soul: the living energy that keeps your body alive, which is still inside Mr. Puss here, hence the purring, and the consciousness energy—the part of your soul that contains your personality and memories. That's the part of Mr. Puss in the jar, and it's also what *you* are made of."

Lifting her hand to amplify her magic, she grabbed on to Cameron with her mind. "A body needs both to stay alive, so let's get you into this pussy before it dies, okay?"

"Yeah. Okay."

Jasmine shoved him into the cat, temporarily fusing his essence with the animal's life energy. As the connection bonded, Cameron-in-cat-form leaped to his feet, arching his back and hissing.

"Calm down. If you're going to be rude, I'll put the cat back together and send you off into the wild." She crossed her arms, leaning against the counter as he lifted his paws, shaking them and flicking his tail, learning to control his new body.

"Row?" He flinched then coughed, opening his mouth wide and making a strangling sound.

"You better not be hacking up a hairball on my countertop."

A low growl formed deep in his throat before he jumped to the floor and sat, blinking up at her. "Ha... Haaa...How?" He shook his head so hard his whole body followed. "How did you do that?"

Jasmine nodded. "Impressive. You're a fast learner to be able to form words with a cat's vocal cords so soon." She pushed from the counter and padded toward her bedroom. "In answer to your question, I'm a necromancer who's learned a little Voodoo magic along the way. I have abilities most don't possess, and that's as far as I'm willing to get into it."

She grabbed her phone from the nightstand and pressed the Home button. "This body will keep *you* safe from the other ghosts and *me* safe from you until the glitch is fixed and the reaper can send you all on your way. Now, let me see if I can get ahold of him again for an update."

The call went straight to voicemail, of course, so she sent Asher a text: *We need to talk.* Crossing her fingers he got his phone fixed, she threw on some clothes and brushed her teeth while the cat sat on the corner of her bed.

The reaper's reply came through as she slipped on her shoes: *Meet me at Sweet Destiny's Bakery.*

"Seriously? He expects me to travel through the swarm of ghosts all the way to the Garden District...for cake?" This right here was why she shouldn't be interested in him anymore. Why she *wasn't* interested. Rolling her eyes, she glanced at Cameron. "I hope you showed a little more concern for other people's well-being while you were alive."

"Not enough or my girlfriend wouldn't have dumped me." He hung his head, giving his new fur a curious look before sticking out his tongue and licking his leg.

"We don't have time for sulking, mister."

"Ack. Why do animals do this? I've got a mouthful of fur." He flicked his little pink tongue in and out, and Jasmine laughed.

"When you figure out you can lick something else, you might not be so grumpy."

He glanced at his belly. "I would never."

"Suuuure…. But listen, if you want my help, you need to get your head in the game. Let's focus on the issue." She typed a response to Asher: *Come to the French Quarter. The ghosts are getting ornery.*

He replied: *In the middle of something. Can't leave.*

It figured. The man wasn't capable of giving a damn about anyone but himself. "C'mon, Mr. Puss. We're going to the Garden District."

Swinging her purse over her shoulder, she opened the front door and stepped onto the sidewalk. The moment her feet hit the pavement, a horde of ghosts surrounded her, all of them shouting and shoving each other, trying to command Jasmine's attention. She had a newfound respect for kindergarten teachers everywhere.

Of course, as they got closer to her personal space, their lack of living energy pulled hers from her body, and cold shivers ran from her head to her toes. Cameron snaked around her feet, arching his back and hissing—which, believe it or not, actually scared some of the spirits away. But there were way more of them than her guard cat could handle, so she stumbled back inside, slammed the door, and marched to her bedroom closet.

"Where are you going?" Cameron followed on her heels. "We can take them."

Her car sat parked in a lot four blocks away, and the protective bubble she created with her mind could only withstand so much pressure. She wouldn't make it that far, even with her new friend's help.

"I appreciate the assistance, but there are just too many of them." It was time to break out the Faraday skirt.

Her invention—created when she was supposed to attend a period costume party at a notoriously haunted plantation—consisted of the innerworkings of a hoop skirt, but made out of aluminum. Suspenders wrapped in foil extended over her shoulders, and she wore aluminum bracelets to help spread the magical shield around her body.

The outfit worked like the aluminum balls strategically placed around the perimeter of her apartment, creating a magical Faraday cage to keep the spirit energy out. The skirt was conveniently collapsible and took up about as much room as a hula hoop in her closet.

She retrieved the skirt cage from behind her Bride of Frankenstein Halloween costume—if a necromancer dressing as someone raised from the dead wasn't funny, she didn't know what was—and stepped into it, hooking the suspenders over her shoulders. Normally, she'd have covered the getup with an antebellum dress to avoid looking like a freak—nobody batted an eye at a person in costume in New Orleans—but it was ninety-eight degrees and one hundred percent humidity outside. She needed to make it to the car without melting.

Besides, she was used to being called a freak; she might as well own it.

She slipped on the bracelets and finished the outfit with a foil-covered headband, complete with a handmade flower accent. Closing her eyes, she activated her protective bubble, sending the magical energy into the metal cage, where it hummed and flowed, creating a barrier that would hold up until she removed the skirt. In theory.

Truth be told, she'd never tried the thing out. Her necromancy services had been requested due to an emergency the night of the costume party, and emergencies paid way too well to pass up.

Of course, the emergency she was facing now wasn't paying squat, but if she didn't help Asher shoo these damn souls across the bridge, she'd never get to leave her house again.

With her magic humming and her attitude tuned to fierce, she picked up the cat and marched out the front door into the throng of ghosts.

"You can see us. Can you help us?" The first ghost floated too close and got zapped by her magical shield. "Ouch!" Her form flickered, becoming more transparent as she backed away.

Jasmine grinned. She was like a walking bug zapper… except for ghosts instead of bugs.

"My business partner owes me money." A man in an expensive suit with a bullet hole in his head drifted toward her. "He stole from me. You have to help." The dude reached for her as if he were going to grab her by the shoulders, and Cameron hissed. The moment the man's ghostly hands touched her forcefield, he jerked back, scowling.

"Money's not going to do you a lick of good where you're headed, buddy." Jasmine's long strides carried her down the street, and the spirits parted, making room for her lest they get electrocuted too.

They gave her room to walk, but as she looked over her shoulder, they'd formed a mass behind her, following her toward the parking lot. That wouldn't do.

"Okay." She spun around and held up her free hand. Hopefully the Faraday skirt would give her commanding magic a boost because she could not deal with all these dead people following her to Magazine Street. "I'm trying to help you, but you cannot keep ambushing me. Stay in the French Quarter. All of you."

She sent out a blast of magic to make the spirits stay put. Then she turned on her heel and ran. The command wouldn't last nearly long enough, and she needed to be as far away as possible before the ghosts returned to their senses and followed her.

Zigzagging up and down the narrow streets, she stopped at a crosswalk and dared a glance behind her. *Thank goodness.* She'd lost the mob for now.

"You really are powerful." Cameron wiggled from her grasp and landed on his feet on the pavement.

"Probably best if you keep quiet in public. Humans can't handle a talking cat, and I don't want the other supes to know about this particular ability of mine. I don't mind hanging out in the gray areas if the price is right, but this…" She gestured to the cat. "This is almost black magic. If I don't put Mr. Puss back together soon, I'll have crossed a line I can't uncross."

The ghost cat sat on his haunches and let out a human-sounding meow.

Jasmine laughed. "That's better. Thank you."

"Nice outfit." A man in a black football jersey sauntered toward her, followed by a group of his friends, as Cameron darted behind her legs.

His sugary-sweet breath smelled of frozen daiquiris, and he tripped as he stepped up to the sidewalk, nearly falling into her. Jasmine took a step back and scooped the cat into her arms, giving the drunk room to faceplant, if that's what he was going for. Sadly, he caught his balance and righted himself.

Even before noon, enough drunks stumbled through the streets to populate an entire rehab facility. It was just her luck she'd stopped to catch her breath on Bourbon Street.

"Lemme get a picture with you." The guy handed his phone to his friend and attempted to wrap an arm around Jasmine's shoulders.

Again, she stepped away, this time into the street. "No thanks. I've got somewhere to be."

"I was going to tip you." He waved a dollar in her face.

"Not interested," she said over her shoulder as she continued on her way.

"Bitch!"

"Whatever." The parking lot stood one block away. She wasn't about to waste time lecturing a drunk man on respect. Anyway, her outfit was outrageous enough that she could understand why tourists might think she was out to make a buck by taking photos. Almost. It wasn't like she'd spray-painted her entire body gold.

She set Cameron on the passenger seat and climbed into her Prius, wrestling with the hoops of her skirt as she attempted to close the door. The biggest hoop blocked it from latching, and it bounced off the ring, jerking from her hand. "Okay, maybe this isn't the best Faraday outfit design I could have come up with." But it was all she had at the moment. She'd make do.

She shimmied the biggest hoop over her head, and the second biggest sat just below her chin. The door would close, and she could reach the steering wheel unencumbered. Good enough.

CHAPTER EIGHT

Navigating the narrow one-way streets of the French Quarter was easier said than done, and Jasmine nearly ran over more than one curious pedestrian who got too close trying to figure out what the hell she was doing sitting behind a wall of metal concentric circles.

She meandered past two- and three-story nineteenth-century buildings in varying shades of blue, yellow, and brown, glancing up at the wrought-iron galleries along the way. She drove slower than all get-out, but such was the way of the French Quarter.

Finally making it past Canal Street, she gunned it, speeding past the modern buildings of the Central Business District until she reached the Garden District. Huge houses dating back to the 1800s replaced the office buildings, and she hung a left toward Magazine Street and Sweet Destiny's Bakery.

She parked and wiggled out of the car, nearly busting her ass on the pavement when a hoop got caught on the seatbelt. After Cameron jumped out, she slammed the door shut and turned in a circle, taking in the beauty of the massive oaks and grand, old houses but also scanning the area for the dead.

She spotted two ghosts across the street, but they didn't pay her any mind, so she strode up the path toward the two-story white wooden Victorian with sky blue shutters that housed Sweet Destiny's Bakery.

"I've been here before." Cameron trotted along beside her. "They have delicious scones."

A bell chimed as she opened the door, and the decadent scents of cinnamon and vanilla wafted to her senses, making her stomach growl. Oh, yeah. She'd skipped breakfast. *Fan-friggin-tastic.*

Cameron paused in the entryway, glancing over his furry shoulder. "Do you mind if I take five minutes to check in on my girlfriend? She lives a block over."

"Remember, Mr. Puss's body is on loan. Don't you dare let her Rottweiler eat it, and if you're not here by the time I leave, you'll have to walk back to the Quarter."

"Yes, ma'am." Cameron darted into the bushes by the porch, disappearing in the brush as Jasmine closed the door and stepped farther inside.

A blonde woman with a cheerful smile and bright blue eyes entered from a back room. "Hi there. I'm Destiny. How can I help you?"

The adrenaline that had been coursing through Jasmine's veins since Cameron knocked on her door this morning dissipated, a calming sensation washing over her as the shop owner moved closer. Jasmine stuttered as the woman's identity registered, her stomach tightening at the realization. "You're...you're an angel."

"Guilty." Destiny tilted her head. "And you're a necromancer. I've never met one of you before."

Her cheeks burned. She had no idea what angels

thought of her kind. Reanimating the dead wasn't exactly a godly business. Or maybe it was too god-like? "There aren't very many of us."

"How can I help you?" The angel's voice lilted with kindness, easing her fear.

"I'm supposed to be meeting Asher here."

Destiny smiled warmly. "He's in the back, helping a friend. Come with me." She paused at the door. "I advise against asking the demon for assistance. He's dying to help, but you won't like the price."

"Um...okay." Based on the number of ghosts roaming the French Quarter, they needed all the help they could get, but who was Jasmine to go against the advice of an angel?

She followed Destiny toward the back room, but the door was narrow, and her hoop wouldn't fit through. Hiking the metal skirt-cage up, she angled it just so until it fit through the door, and then let it fall back into place.

Asher sat at the table with a demon who had dark hair and glowing red eyes. As the demon put a piece of angel food cake into his mouth, the red dimmed to a dark brown, and he relaxed his right hand, which was clenched in a fist.

"I'm so sorry, Mike. I had no idea being in hell would affect you this bad." Asher rubbed Mike's back, the worry in his eyes making him appear almost empathetic, as if the man who cared about nothing but his job actually cared about another person's well-being.

"It's all right. I'm glad I could help." Mike ate another bite of cake, and Asher stared at the chocolate slice on the plate in front of him. It hadn't been touched.

"I feel awful."

He did? The block of concrete Jasmine had erected

around her heart crumbled a little. Not entirely, but Asher's expression held genuine concern…an emotion she'd convinced herself he was incapable of feeling.

"It's okay. I'm getting better by the bite." Mike looked up and caught Jasmine's gaze, his hand curling into a fist again. "I think someone's here to see you."

Asher followed Mike's gaze and shot to his feet as he saw her. "Jasmine." He swallowed hard, giving her a once-over, and then a second look. "What are you wearing? I mean…thanks for coming. This is Mike. He's…"

"I'm just leaving. Crimson's on her way over, so I'll be at my place if you need anything else." He turned toward the door but paused, looking over his shoulder. "Anything that doesn't involve the underworld."

"Right. I'll take it from here. Thanks again." Asher waved goodbye as Mike exited through the back, and then he pulled out a chair for Jasmine. "Do you want to sit?"

She did, and that slice of chocolate cake sitting on the table called to her like O negative to a vampire. But… "My outfit isn't great for sitting. Or driving. Or anything really. It's very poorly designed."

He fought a smile. "What exactly is the purpose? It's…interesting."

"It's to protect me from all the ghosts you've turned loose in the French Quarter. There are hundreds of them. You know that, right?"

"Closer to a thousand, I think." He cleared his throat. "A necromancer who's afraid of ghosts…? How does that protect you?"

"I'm not afraid of them. They're annoying." She wasn't about to share her little weakness with an immortal being. Especially this one. "It's like a Faraday cage; it blocks spirit energy." Her eyebrows shot up as his words finally registered. "A thousand?" *Holy ghost guts.* "Why didn't you tell me it was so bad?"

He sank into the chair and picked up a fork, sinking it into that decadent-looking cake. "I tried. You were pretty short with me last night."

"I was…" She wanted to argue, but what could she say? She had been short with him. She'd acted like a bitch, but he'd broken her heart without a hint of explanation. He didn't deserve friendliness.

"I understand." He took a bite of cake, chewing and swallowing before he continued. "You have every reason in the world to hate me. I haven't exactly been easy to get along with since…"

Something about the way he'd been talking to Mike and the way he looked at her now made him seem vulnerable. Almost human. She needed to find some better building material because her heart wall wouldn't last long like this.

"Where's Mike?" Destiny's voice sounded from behind her. "I just baked a fresh batch with a little extra magic in them."

"Your cake is magic?" Thankful for the distraction, Jasmine turned toward her.

"Only the angel food cake. It helps the recovering demons stay in recovery." She set the box on a counter. "Can I get you something?"

"That chocolate cake looks good." And maybe if her mouth was full it would stop her from plying Asher with questions she no longer wanted the answers to.

"One slice of devil's food cake coming up. Have a seat, and I'll bring it right out."

"Um…" Jasmine looked at her skirt. "Do you get many ghosts in here?"

"Not at all. You're safe." Destiny scurried to the kitchen, and Jasmine unhooked the skirt from her suspenders, letting it collapse to the floor.

"Why are there a thousand ghosts in the French Quarter, but hardly any out here?" She stepped out of the hoops and sank into a chair. "Did the people in hell get the glitch fixed, because I can't handle all these spirits following me around. They know I can see them, which makes me like a lighthouse to the dead."

"About that…" He toyed with his fork.

"What glitch?" Destiny returned with the cake and set it on the table.

"The glitch that locked the doors to the underworld." Jasmine looked at Asher. "I assume that's why you had the demon take you to hell, right? To fix the glitch?" She took a bite of cake, and lord have mercy, it was like heaven found a new home on her tongue. Rich and moist, the bittersweet chocolate melded with the creamy frosting perfectly. She had another bite before Asher could even answer.

"It's not exactly a glitch. It's more like a failsafe. I got a new phone, though, so that's good." He held up the device.

Destiny picked up the box of angel food cake. "She doesn't know?"

"Not exactly."

Jasmine took another bite of blissful cake, her gaze bouncing between the reaper and the angel as they conversed.

"You should tell her." Destiny rested a hand on his shoulder, inhaling deeply as if receiving some kind of divine message. "Tell her everything. Your fears are unfounded, and they're holding you back from your destiny."

"My destiny…" Asher blinked, wariness tightening his eyes.

"I'm going to take these over to Mike. Have a nice chat, you two." The angel winked and slipped out the door.

"What was that about?" Jasmine shoved another massive bite of chocolate cake into her mouth. "Good call meeting here, by the way. This is decadent."

"Um…" Asher seemed puzzled as he raked a hand through his light blond hair.

"What are you supposed to tell me?"

He looked at her, the muscles in his jaw working as he ground his teeth, his expression pinching as if he were working out some inner conflict in his mind.

Her throat thickened as his pale blue eyes held hers. He wasn't looking at her, but into her, like he could actually see her life energy. *Holy soul stealers*, the man was intense. She swallowed. "What's going on?"

He let out a heavy breath, nodding with resolve. "I know you think I'm an asshole after everything that happened, and I think I should explain…"

Her pulse sprinted. Her heart was completely unprepared for the *it's not you, it's me* talk. She'd come here to discuss ghosts, not *the incident*. She wasn't ready for this. *Deflect, Jazz! Deflect!* "What's there to explain? The chief of police wanted to speak to a high-profile criminal after he was murdered, and I was supposed to make that happen. I *promised* to make that happen, but I couldn't deliver because someone decided his own job was more important than mine."

Yes, she'd focus on work. Let him think *the incident* wasn't a big deal and she was only mad about work.

Asher closed his eyes for a long blink. "I didn't take that soul from you just to be a dick after you kissed me."

Christ on a cracker! Could the guy not take a hint? Well, if he insisted on talking about it… "It sure seemed like you did. You could've just told me you weren't interested, you know? That's what a decent man would do."

"It's not that I'm…" His nostrils flared as he blew out another breath. "I took it because it was a high priority. He'd reneged on a deal with Satan, and I had a deadline to meet. When I don't do my job, disastrous things happen."

"I know it's your job, but you could've given me ten minutes. I just needed the guy to give the police some information." She took another bite, talking around the cake in her mouth. "It was a high priority for me too. The chief was livid when I couldn't make the corpse talk."

"I know. But he was being summoned to the bowels of hell. One of the worst punishment levels aside from the tarpits, and I couldn't let him have access to a body, even for ten minutes. You have no idea the bad deeds he'd done."

She lifted one shoulder. "I might have if you'd let me talk to him."

"He would have tried to kill you."

Wait. Asher had whisked in and snatched the soul from her grasp because he was trying to protect her? Her shoulders drooped, and the wall around her heart crumbled a little more before she could compose herself. She didn't need protecting. "I could have yanked him out of the corpse as fast as I put him in if that were the case. Dead people inside bodies can't hurt me." And *one* ghost without a body couldn't either. She could have shoved it back into the aether, easy peasy.

"Point taken. I'll try to care less about your safety in the future." His fork clinked on the plate as he mashed it into the cake before shoving it into his mouth.

"That's funny." Suddenly without an appetite, she pushed her plate away. "You don't care about me, and you've proven it." She couldn't let herself get sucked back into believing she might have a future with a being from hell. Perhaps he was trying to protect her that time, but he still ghosted her.

"I do care."

"Whatever." He couldn't atone for two months of the silent treatment with one conversation.

His hands clenched into fists on the table before he gave his head a tiny shake and sighed. "Can I explain what happened with my door, please? I assume since you came all the way out here in a hoop skirt and tin foil helmet that you're planning to help?"

"It's aluminum, and it's not a helmet. I'm not blocking aliens or government mind-reading devices. Just ghosts."

He chuckled. "Gotcha. Well, the ghosts are my fault, and if you're still willing to help, I would appreciate it."

"How are they your fault? You said it was a glitch." She pulled her plate back in front of her. She wasn't *completely* without an appetite after all.

As she polished off her cake, he told her a story about being on a beach in Aruba for the past two weeks and how he'd set up a lamp filled with sun fairy light to allow the dead to take a self-guided trip to the underworld. "The problem is, reapers aren't allowed to take vacations."

"Then, why did you?"

He stared at his plate. "I had a lot on my mind."

"Like?"

He opened his mouth to say something but then closed it again as if he'd changed his mind. She'd never seen the guy so indecisive. "There are forces at play in my life that I can't even begin to explain."

"Try."

"I can't." He shoved a bite of cake into his mouth.

She drummed her nails on the table, frustration gnawing in her stomach. But hey, at least they weren't talking about *the incident* anymore. "Fine. I'm guessing your porch light plan didn't work?"

"It worked for a few days, until someone escaped."

"Escaped?" She blinked. *Yikes.* "You let a soul escape from the underworld? Please tell me it was a nice spirit. Someone who'll go back willingly if you ask?"

He laughed, but there wasn't any humor in it. "It was Jean Lafitte."

"*The* Jean—"

"Yeah. Not the nicest guy. Most pirates aren't, and believe me, he will not go back willingly. He was the toughest soul I've ever reaped."

"I saw a pirate at the bar last night." That had to be Lafitte. He was the first ghost to ever slip from her grasp.

"It figures. I didn't know who I was looking for then, but if I'd seen him, it would have saved me a trip to hell and Mike a whole mess of trouble." With an elbow on the table, he rested his head in his hand.

"Is he going to be okay? His eyes were scary when I walked in."

"He will be. He's a recovering demon, and being in hell tempted him to go back to his old ways. Destiny used her angel magic to calm him down."

"Can her angel magic help catch an ornery ghost?"

"Sadly, no. And I've been instructed not to let anyone else associated with the underworld find out what happened. Not unless I want to be thrown in the tarpits."

Seeing him like this, vulnerable and concerned about his friend, sharing his epic screw-up with her, the final piece of her wall crumbled, the anger falling away and leaving nothing but the raw pain of rejection behind.

It was a good thing, making it past the anger stage of her grief, but *holy agony* it hurt. Being mad was so much easier.

"If I help you catch Lafitte, you'll be able to unlock your door and then take all the ghosts with you?"

He nodded slowly. "In theory. The problem is, the longer my door is locked, the weaker I'm becoming. My magic flows from the underworld through my door. It's only a matter of time before I don't have enough power to make it to the threshold, much less unlock it."

"Well, then we better get busy. I think I might know where we can find your pirate."

CHAPTER NINE

Asher watched Jasmine out of the corner of his eye as she drove toward the French Quarter. She'd insisted on wearing her ridiculous metal skirt out of the bakery, but he'd convinced her to take it off for the drive.

Why a woman with her power thought she needed protection from ghosts, he had no clue. If she wanted to, she could line all thousand of them up and have them doing burpees at her command. She'd told him something similar not too long ago. Deep down, she underestimated herself, but Jasmine was the most powerful necromancer he'd ever met.

He was about to question her again about the reason for the outfit when an orange cat jumped onto the console between them. Asher gasped, his heart moving north, threatening to leap from his throat, while the contents of his bladder attempted to move south. *Satan's balls!* Had it been in the back seat the entire time, and he'd been too distracted by the beautiful woman beside him to notice? Thankfully, he got his bodily urges under control before he made even more of an ass of himself, but Jasmine didn't so much as flinch.

She patted the cat on the head before returning both hands to the steering wheel. "I hope you found what you were looking for."

The cat let out a meow that sounded more like a human groan and settled in the back seat.

"Sorry about that," Jasmine said over her shoulder. "I know you're looking for closure, but sometimes it just doesn't come."

"Cute cat." He peered at the animal in the back seat. From the way she spoke to it, he'd wager it was more than a mundane feline, though. "Since when do necromancers keep familiars?"

"What's a familiar?" the cat asked.

Asher narrowed his eyes at Jasmine. "And since when do familiars talk?"

She cleared her throat. "That's Cameron. He's a ghost friend of mine. It seems your lost souls are devouring each other, so I put him in a cat to keep him safe."

Did he hear that right? "You took a human soul and just…stuffed him inside a cat?"

"Yep."

"How did…?" He eyed the cat again, lifting his nose and searching for the telltale sickly-sweet scents of death. He didn't find any, not even the slightest hint of decay. "That's a living animal. Does the cat realize he's being… occupied? How did you even get a second soul inside?"

She drummed her fingers on the steering wheel. "It's kind of a murky, gray area of necromancy. Are you sure you want me to explain?"

He looked at the man-cat, who seemed as content as a dead guy inside a feline body could be, and his admiration of Jasmine's power grew. Was there anything this woman couldn't do? "Best if I don't know, then."

"I think that's a wise choice."

"What are we doing, by the way?" Cameron tucked his paws beneath his chest. "My girlfriend wasn't home, so I missed the whole plan for nothing. We do have a plan, right?"

Jasmine filled the cat in on everything they'd discussed, Asher's ears burning as she relayed the story. "Now New Orleans is overrun with ghosts, and if we don't fix it soon, there'll be hell to pay."

"Let me get this straight," Cameron said. "The longer it takes to find the pirate, the weaker your reaper power becomes." He looked at Jasmine. "And *you* get—"

"More and more irritated the longer you keep talking?" She narrowed her eyes at the cat in the rearview mirror. "You're all caught up, so let's have some peace and quiet for a few minutes, shall we?"

Asher stared out the windshield, trying to ignore the way being near her made his heart race, but his attempt was futile. She'd always had this effect on him, and it seemed she always would. His two weeks in Aruba had done nothing to diminish the space this woman had carved for herself in his heart. He didn't know why or how he ended up being *that* reaper, but he couldn't deny his feelings for her anymore. No matter how far away he got, Jasmine would always be with him.

As they made it to the French Quarter, she parked the car in a lot a few blocks from Bourbon Street and fastened her hoop skirt to the suspenders. "You're not going to be too embarrassed to be seen with me like this, are you?"

Beneath the metal getup, she wore black shorts with combat boots and a dark red tank top that clung to her curves. He stepped back to admire her, his lips tugging into a smile against his will. "You actually look kinda hot. A little steampunk mixed with modern feminism. I like it."

She froze, her mask of indifference slipping for a fraction of a second before she glared at him. "You don't get to say things like that to me. Not after you rejected me."

She marched out of the parking lot, deeper into the Quarter, and Asher stood still, watching her walk away.

"Someone pissed off the necromancer." Cameron jumped onto the hood of the car. "What happened?"

Asher shook his head. "I was an idiot."

"It's none of my business, but I watched her yank a soul from a living thing and shove it into a jar. Immortal being or not, I wouldn't want to get on her bad side. You are immortal, right? How old are you?"

"Two-hundred-something," Asher mumbled as he jogged to catch up. "I didn't reject you, Jasmine."

"No?" She whirled around to face him. "I told you I liked you, so you ripped a portal in the air and disappeared through it. If that's not rejection, I don't know what is." She continued her march toward Bourbon Street. "And we've already discussed what a jerk you've been ever since."

"We've hardly spoken since." Because he had no idea what to say. She'd caught him off-guard with that kiss, and he'd freaked. She had no idea the severity of what could be happening between them, and he had no idea what to do about it. Once he gave his heart to her, he couldn't take it back… Even if she decided she didn't want it anymore.

"Whoa." She stopped on the corner next to a musician who was blissfully unaware of the ghostly audience watching him play his saxophone.

Hundreds of spirits mingled with the living on New Orleans' most famous street. Music blared from inside the clubs, and hawkers with Big Ass Beer signs shouted at passersby, trying to get them into their establishments, completely oblivious to the dead floating among them.

"Do they look unusually solid for being in the daylight?" Asher squeezed his eyes shut and opened them again, but the spirits all looked nearly opaque. This was not good.

Jasmine wiped a drop of sweat from her brow. "They sure do."

"Who?" Cameron pawed at her leg. "What are you looking at? I can't see spirits when I'm in this body. What's happening?"

"What did I tell you about using words in public?" She gave the cat a pointed look before casting her gaze to her surroundings.

"Meow?" he said in a very humanlike tone.

"There are ghosts everywhere, and they're strong." She made eye contact with a spirit, and it rushed her.

Asher grabbed his pen, though what he'd do with his scythe on a busy public street, he wasn't sure. Jasmine didn't need his help, though. The second the ghost brushed against her ghost-repelling skirt, it got an electrical zap and backed away.

"I'm impressed." He nodded his appreciation. "That's quite an invention."

She looked into his eyes, her own softening for a moment before she composed herself. "If I were a pirate escapee just returned to town, I'd be checking out all my old haunts. That's the one he's most famous for, so I say we start there." She nodded toward an eighteenth-century building across the street. Two attic windows jutted upward from the sagging roof, and open green shutters lined the windows and doors of the brick and plaster façade.

"Sounds like a plan." Asher followed her to the entrance, and Cameron darted inside.

"Aww…a kitty." A woman reached down to pet him, and Jasmine rolled her eyes.

"At least he's distracting the humans. C'mon." As she motioned inside, Asher stepped through the door.

A brick hearth occupied the center of the L-shaped room, its chimney extending through the exposed wood ceiling, and a bar lined the short arm of the L, while tables dotted the floor along the long side.

The owner, a six-foot-tall gator shifter named Buck, stood frozen behind the bar, his mouth hanging open as he stared at the piano in the back of the room. Classical music drifted on the air as the keys—to everyone else's eyes—seemed to be moving on their own.

"That's not a player piano," Buck whispered, locking his wide brown eyes on Asher. "Is it..?"

Asher nodded. "We'll take care of it."

The notorious pirate sat on the bench, playing the background music in a building he used to own. His form was completely solid, his grayscale palette the only thing giving him away as a ghost. That and the fact that no one else knew he was even there.

"What's the plan?" Jasmine cracked her knuckles. "You just hit him with your scythe and send him packing?"

Asher backed away slowly. If the ghost sensed his presence, he'd bolt before he could get the pen from his pocket. "We need a distraction. If we act fast enough, we can portal him away before the patrons notice, but not if anyone is looking directly at us."

"How fast do we have to be?" Jasmine scanned the crowd behind them. The bar was packed, as usual.

"Too fast. If we'd have waited 'til nightfall, we could have asked Gaston to glamour them, but I don't want to miss this chance."

Jasmine's lip curled. "I don't work with vampires."

"Why not?"

"They're undead." She shrugged. "They're attracted to my power over souls, and I'm too tempted to rip theirs out and let their bodies die all the way like they should have to begin with. Nothing personal."

"Gotcha. No vampires then." Asher rolled the pen in his hand, trying to formulate a plan.

Cameron meandered back toward them, sitting at Jasmine's feet, and she nodded. "Hey, Cam, can you distract the humans for a minute while we nab this ghost? I'm talking John Wick-level distraction."

"You...want me to kill them all?"

"No!" Asher shook his head adamantly.

Jasmine laughed. "Just get their fists flying. A brawl, if you will. If they're busy wailing on each other, they won't notice what we're doing."

Cameron glanced at the crowd before looking up at her. "I've never been in a bar fight before."

"Now's your chance."

"I'm on it." He prowled to the front of the room and hopped on a table, letting out a wicked hiss and swatting a paw at one of the patrons. The woman screamed, shooting to her feet and knocking over her chair before dumping her beer over her shoulder onto the person behind her.

The man stood, drawing his fist back as if ready to strike, and the woman's date darted around the table to throw the first punch instead.

With everyone's attention on the cat's disaster, Asher rushed up behind the pirate, extending his scythe as he moved. Lafitte stopped playing, and in a blur of light, he shot to the other side of the grand piano, a big shit-eating grin on his ashy face.

Well, it was more like a ghost-eating grin, since he'd apparently turned into an energy vampire. And how the hell did he move like that?

"What are you doing out of hell, Lafitte?"

The pirate leaned a hand on the piano and laughed. "Dead men tell no tales."

"Seriously?" Jasmine scoffed. "Can you be any more cliché?"

"Batten down the hatches, lass. I'm not going to make this easy on your reaper."

"You don't have to." Asher stepped onto the bench and leaped onto the piano, sliding across the polished black surface. He swiped his scythe at Lafitte as his feet hit the floor, but the damn pirate disintegrated, reforming in a doorway leading to a back room.

"Need some help?" Jasmine knocked over a chair with her hoop skirt on her way toward him.

"Can you hold him still?"

"I'll try."

Lafitte laughed again and disappeared through the doorway.

"Dammit." Asher ran toward the door, but Jasmine's skirt got caught on a loose brick in the fireplace. She yanked so hard, the aluminum ring bent, but the hearth wouldn't let go. He turned toward her to help her break free, but she waved him on.

"Go after him. I'll catch up."

When he hesitated, she yelled, "Go!"

He shot through the door after his mark and found Lafitte standing near a supply shelf, clutching a semi-transparent spirit in his hands. As he gripped the ghost's shoulders, it began to fade, becoming more and more translucent as he drained its energy.

Satan would not be happy to receive a bunch of lifeless ghosts. He needed their energy to power hell, not to fuel an ancient pirate.

Asher clutched his scythe like a baseball bat. "C'mon, Lafitte. It's time to go home."

The pirate released his ghost victim, who disappeared through the wall, and he inclined his chin. "It's not time. I'm on a mission, and I won't abandon ship." He floated upward, then his face contorted with a look of surprise as he was yanked downward. "Shiver me timbers!"

"Yo ho ho, it's a pirate's life for me." Jasmine stepped into the room, shaking her head. "I can't believe I just said that." Her foil suspenders slipped from her shoulders as she raised her hands toward Lafitte. Her skirt was gone, no doubt tangled in the fireplace, but she obviously didn't need it. She'd nabbed the soul a two-hundred-something-year-old reaper couldn't catch. *Wow.*

"I've got you this time." Her boots thudded on the wood floor as she walked closer to the spirit.

"Do ye, though?" Lafitte arched a brow and jerked his shoulders as if yanking from her grasp. Then he rushed her. He was on her before Asher could even blink, knocking her to the ground and hovering above her. "You need to learn a little humility, wench."

Jasmine gasped, her body convulsing as the ghost turned his energy-draining power on her.

Asher planted his foot in the side of Lafitte's head, knocking him off Jasmine. With his scythe, he tore open a portal and whisked her through, away from the ghost and into her living room.

Her eyes rolled backward, and she moaned as he laid her on the couch. "Holy Hades, that hurt."

"Are you okay?"

"I will be. Just give me a minute." She closed her eyes and lay still, her breathing slowing as her body relaxed.

What had he done? His idiotic plan to get away and find himself, rather than accepting his fate and making his destiny happen, had resulted in the one person he could actually have a life with nearly being killed by a ghost.

A life. As if his current existence didn't count as living. If he were honest with himself, he'd admit it didn't. He'd admit he was *that* reaper, and he wanted to share his life with someone. To experience love.

He gazed at Jasmine lying on the couch, watching the rise and fall of her chest as she breathed. Was he willing to give up his immortality for her...for the chance to be happy?

Her eyes moved beneath her closed lids, and he kneeled on the floor beside her, brushing a stray strand of hair off her forehead. "Jasmine?"

Her lips parted on a quick breath, and her lids fluttered open.

"What the...?" Jasmine blinked, her blurry vision focusing on Asher's handsome features. He kneeled beside her, his face hovering inches above hers, concern etching lines into his forehead. She inhaled deeply, and his warm, rugged scent reminded her of a campfire on a summer evening.

His gaze dipped briefly to her lips before he sat back

on his heels and swallowed hard. "Are you sure you're okay?"

"Um…" She rubbed her forehead before rising onto her elbows. When the room stopped spinning, she pushed to a sitting position and rested her feet on the floor. *Her* floor. She glanced around the room, confusion clouding her mind. The last thing she remembered was lying on the cold concrete in the back room of the pub, a pirate ghost sucking the life energy out of her.

"I portaled you here." Asher sat on the sofa next to her. "Lafitte was attacking you, and I…"

"Thank you." She searched his eyes, trying to believe what her heart told her was true. The key to unlocking his door and solving all his problems was within his grasp, but he'd chosen to save her rather than continue fighting the pirate. She didn't know he was capable of such kindness. Maybe Asher was different after all.

"What happened in there? You said you could line up all the spirits and make them do the limbo, but it looked like Lafitte had you as low as you can go."

She wanted to be offended, but the worry in his eyes defused her ego. "I said that when I thought we were dealing with a dozen normal ghosts, not some super spirit who can siphon the energy from others, and definitely not a thousand of them."

"Most of the others are recently deceased, so they won't be that strong."

"It doesn't matter if they died five minutes or five years ago, if they get too close, they suck the energy from me like a tourist sucking down a Pat O'Brien's hurricane." She clamped her mouth shut. Dammit, she didn't mean to tell him that.

"Wait. All spirits can do that to you? Not just the strong ones?"

Resting her elbows on her knees, she held her head in her hands. "Why do you think necromancers reanimate corpses rather than dealing directly with ghosts?"

"I thought it was so other people could talk to the dead. And maybe to show off a little."

She sat up straight. "You think reanimating the dead is to show off?"

"It is a pretty cool talent. What you did with Cameron is too."

"Cool?" She rose to her feet, and the room tipped on its side. Pressing a hand to her head, she reached her other arm out, hoping to grip the wall or a shelf. Instead, her palm landed flat against Asher's shoulder as he stood to steady her.

"Whoa there." He gently gripped her elbows. "Maybe you should lie down and rest? How long does it take to recover from an attack like that?"

"I'm fine. A few hours' sleep, and I'll be like new." She swatted him away. The last thing she needed was the feel of his hard muscles beneath her fingers making her head spin for another reason. "And since when do you think my magic is cool? Last I heard, you thought it was disgusting, just like everyone else."

He dropped his arms to his sides. "I never said I thought it was disgusting."

"You never said you didn't." Her stomach turned, and she gripped her abdomen.

"Well, I don't."

"What then? Why…?" She wanted to ask him why he ran out that night. Why he hadn't said more than two words to her since it happened. But her vision tunneled, and the next thing she knew, she was waking up to the sound of a purring tomcat curled up next to her in bed.

Soft morning sunlight filtered in through the blinds, making Cameron-in-cat-form's orange fur shimmer. His warmth seeped into her hip, and she angled her head, smiling as she watched him sleep. She was going to miss him when this was all over. Once the ornery tomcat's soul took over the body again, he'd probably go back to spraying her porch and using her plant pots as a litter box.

She lay her head back on the pillow and stared at the ceiling fan hanging stagnant above. She normally turned it on high when she went to bed. Summer in New Orleans was like hell on Earth, and the old AC unit had seen better days. Why didn't she turn it on last night?

Come to think of it, she didn't even remember coming to bed. And how did Cameron get inside? Asher had portaled them here, but they'd left the cat behind. The ghost pirate had drained her more than anything she'd ever felt. She remembered talking to Asher while she lay on the couch. Then she got up and stumbled... Had Asher brought her to bed?

Her chest warmed at the thought of him being in her bedroom. But where was he now? Making breakfast in her kitchen? Wouldn't that be something? The way he looked at her yesterday... He'd saved her life, missed his target, and he didn't seem the slightest bit upset about it. He almost seemed like he cared.

Her lips tugged into a grin. He also called her necromancy ability "cool." It wasn't a profession of undying love, but it was a start. Whatever his reason for portaling away after *the incident*, it wasn't because he found her disgusting.

She sat up, listening for sounds of anyone else in her

apartment, but all she heard was a car passing outside and Cameron's contented purring.

"Asher?" she called into the emptiness. He didn't respond.

Cameron stirred at the sound of her voice. "I missed you, Isabelle." He rubbed his head against her hip, stretching out onto his side. If cats could smile, he'd have been grinning from ear to ear. She hated to rouse him from his dream world, but her memory of the night had too many blank spots.

"Wake up, Cam." She put her hand on his soft fur and gave him a little shake.

He blinked his eyes open, lifting his head before dropping it back on the mattress with a groan. "You're not Isabelle."

"Sorry to disappoint."

He rose onto his paws, arching his back and stretching his legs. "What's disappointing is the fact that you left me alone in the middle of a bar fight. Do you have any idea how humiliating it is to be picked up by the scruff of your neck and thrown into the street? Luckily this cat likes your back porch. I used his instincts or whatever to find my way here."

"How'd you get inside?"

"Asher let me in. You've been asleep since yesterday afternoon."

"Where is he now?"

"Hopefully at home sleeping too. Did you know even immortals have to sleep? He said he only needs a couple of hours, but I would have thought if you live forever, you wouldn't need rest."

"He left." Her shoulders slumped as she blew out a breath. Of course he left. To hope otherwise was lunacy.

Even if he were capable of human emotions, he was married to his job, and Jasmine refused to be a mistress. "Typical."

"Do you have any food? I'm starving." Cameron jumped to the floor.

"I could use some fuel myself. Let me see what I can whip up." She slid out of bed and shuffled to the kitchen.

"You said it's typical that Asher left." He climbed into a chair and leaped onto the countertop. "Typical of what? Men?"

She pursed her lips. "I guess. More like typical of him." She took a carton of eggs from the fridge and set a frying pan on the stove. "He's a reaper. I shouldn't expect him to have normal emotions, but sometimes..." Shaking her head, she cracked the eggs and scrambled them.

Cameron padded toward her, nudging her arm with his head. "Sometimes what?"

"Why does it matter?"

"Humor me? I honestly have no idea why Isabelle dumped me. Help me understand the female mind." He sat on his haunches. "You stuffed me into a cat. It's the least you can do."

"I..." She started to argue she saved him from the cannibal spirits, but the man didn't need a reminder he was dead. Dumping the eggs into the pan, she stirred them with a wooden spoon. "Sometimes, when he looks at me a certain way, I feel... I feel like he cares. I shouldn't. He's made it clear he's not interested in me, but a girl can dream, right?"

"He cares." Cam leaped gracefully to the floor and returned to the table.

"What makes you say that?" Jasmine put the eggs on the plates and set one in front of him.

Cameron dove into the food, smacking his little cat mouth as he devoured everything on his plate. Jasmine took a bite of her eggs, trying to wait patiently, but *furious felines*, that cat could eat.

When he finished licking every morsel from the surface, he finally lifted his head. "He sat in a chair by your bed all night. The guy looked rough. I finally convinced him to leave and let me watch over you. He could hardly keep his eyes open."

"Really?" Her stomach fluttered at the idea. "He watched over me all night? That's...creepy." And utterly romantic. Ugh. It was better when she hated him. Now she felt all warm and mushy inside, and she didn't do warm and mushy...probably because she'd never gotten close enough to anyone for her insides to heat and soften.

"I guess what I was doing, sneaking around Isabelle's house, was creepy too, huh?" Cameron asked.

"A little bit, yeah."

He sighed. "I should have talked to her more. Just told her how I felt rather than trying to play it cool. I deserved what happened."

"No." She started to pet him, but there was a human man inside that little kitty body. Instead, she took his paw in her hand. "No one deserves to die. You made a mistake. Sadly, you're paying the ultimate price."

"Well, lucky for you, both you and Asher are alive. I think. Are reapers alive? Anyway, you should talk to him."

"Maybe." She would like to know what happened between them...at least get some closure if he truly wasn't into her. She could handle that, couldn't she? Perhaps. Not really. Honestly, with a thousand ghosts on the loose, neither of them needed the distraction.

"Later. We've got a pirate to catch first."

CHAPTER TEN

Asher checked his hair in the mirror one more time before extending his scythe and preparing to portal to Jasmine's apartment. She'd asked questions yesterday before she passed out. Well, she'd also made accusations, but she deserved answers. Especially to her question of why.

Fear was his best answer, though admitting his fear to a woman who would jump into a pit of crocodiles to wrestle the one who looked at her funny wasn't exactly good for his reputation. He was the embodiment of Death itself, yet he was afraid of it. How ironic was that?

Of course, he was also afraid of love. Not so much the emotion, but of what would happen if she ever saw him in his true form. How could a strong, vivacious woman ever love a man who was literally designed to strike fear in the hearts of the wicked?

Okay, maybe he was afraid of rejection too.

But Jasmine deserved to know. To know everything. Well, almost everything. She didn't need to see his true form, but he would tell her how he felt about her and about the consequences they'd face if he gave his heart to her.

He nodded, resolved to stop playing games, and portaled into her living room.

Jasmine sat on the sofa next to Cameron, her thumbs hovering above the screen of her phone. "There you are. I was afraid you'd gotten lost." She leaned onto her hip to shove her phone into her pocket.

Asher reached a hand into the gateway before it closed, pulling one side away like a curtain so she could look through. "Kinda hard to lose my way, wouldn't you say?"

She stood, a look of wonder in her eyes as she stepped toward him and peered through the hole. "Wow. Is that your living room?" Her reverent whisper raised the hairs on the back of his neck, and he closed his eyes to enjoy the floral scent of her shampoo, the warmth radiating from her body.

"Is that a picture of a kitten hanging from a tree branch on the wall in there?"

He jerked his hand out, letting the portal slam shut, and shrank his scythe to pen-size. "I like cats...and the message."

"Who am I to judge?" She held up her hands and smirked at Cameron. "Death likes to 'Hang in there, baby.' The kitten looks like a younger version of you, Cam."

"I'm still trying to wrap my mind around y'all even existing. I'm not judging either of you."

Asher glanced around the room to find something to tease Jasmine about, to shift the focus to her, but he found nothing. Her light beige walls held black and white photographs of flowers and landscapes, and a shelf filled with books sat next to a small entertainment center.

Everything about her—aside from her ability—was so normal. His throat thickened. She definitely could not see his true form. Ever.

"So, what's the plan?" She dropped onto the pale blue sofa and crossed her legs. "Lafitte is obviously stronger than either one of us thought, if our last encounter is any indication."

"About that." He shoved his hands in his pockets, his stomach tightening into a knot. "You asked me some questions yesterday, and I—"

She waved a hand. "Ravings of a madwoman. I was out of my mind, so forget about it."

"But—"

"The most important thing right now is getting your door unlocked so nothing like that happens again. To me or any other necromancers out there, who, by the way, wouldn't be happy to know that I spilled our little weakness secret to you. So keep it quiet, okay?"

"You're right, and your secret is safe with me." Of course she was right. Neither one of them would survive much longer if they didn't take care of the problem at hand. Talking would have to wait. "We need another plan. I've tried locating him the usual way I do when a name appears on my list, but he's disguising his energy."

"It's probably because he's consuming the other ghosts. Their energy is mixing with his, making him stronger and harder to find."

Asher sank into the chair next to the sofa. "Maybe we could try together? I assume your location magic works in a similar way to mine, right? If we combine our power, then maybe we can find him."

Jasmine shook her head. "I need something that belonged to the spirit. Sometimes a living relative will work, but most of the time I have to use an object the spirit possessed in life to read the energy. Otherwise, I can't tell who's who."

Cameron stopped licking his paws to look at her. "What of mine did you use? I didn't see any of my possessions in the morgue."

She laughed. "I had an object you never left home without. Your body!"

"Oh." He lowered his furry brow. "Well, if I'm not mistaken, Jean Lafitte was buried at sea, so unless you've got some SCUBA gear…"

"We need something that belonged to him." Asher tapped a finger against his chin. "What about the bar?"

"Buildings are too detached. Too much other energy has passed through. I need something more personal: a book, a tankard, a weapon."

"Do you think they'd have something at the bar that belonged to him?"

"It's worth a shot." She grinned. "Can you portal us there? I've never been through one while conscious."

He hesitated to do it. Between the fatigue after staying up most of the night to watch over her, then searching the French Quarter for the pirate, and the dull throb at the back of his head, he needed to conserve his energy. But the excitement in her eyes burrowed into his heart, planting roots there and making it impossible for him to deny her.

Pulling his pen from his pocket, he clicked the plunger, and it magically extended into his scythe. He pictured the supply closet in the back room and sliced through the air, creating an opening to the bar that lay four blocks away. "After you, m'lady."

He gestured to the opening, and her smile widened, making his heart beat faster. She stepped through without hesitation, the look of awe in her eyes turning his heart to mush.

"Are you coming?" he asked Cameron.

The cat eyed the portal. "I think I'll sit this one out, if you don't mind. I've had about all the weirdness I can handle for now. You two have fun."

"I understand." Asher stepped through the gateway, and it closed behind him.

"Oh, no. Not you again." The bar owner hoisted a keg onto his shoulder like it weighed nothing and blocked the supply closet exit. "You caused enough trouble yesterday."

"Trouble?" Jasmine fisted her hands on her hips. "We saved your establishment from a ghost who's looking for more trouble than you can handle."

"It was playing the piano. *You* caused a brawl." His voice was low and gravelly, filled with warning that Jasmine ignored.

She pointed a finger and invaded his personal space, though she had to crane her neck to look up into his face. "You have no idea—"

"We're so sorry about the trouble, Buck." Asher placed a hand on her arm, gently tugging her toward him. The last thing they needed was to see this mountain of a man shift into an enormous gator with a million teeth. "I need to escort the spirit to the underworld, and we're having trouble catching him. He's a pirate, and we were hoping you might have some items that belonged to Jean Lafitte. His energy might help me locate my mark."

A proud smile tugged at Buck's lips. "I have plenty of items."

Jasmine softened her voice, following Asher's lead. "May we see them?"

It took some convincing, but the bartender offered

them a selection of tankards, a shoehorn, and an old knife. Asher held each one, trying to mimic Jasmine's grip to see if he could feel the energy of the former owner. As expected, he felt nothing. His ability to locate his spirit marks came from the underworld, through his doorway. With it locked, he couldn't tell Lafitte's essence from a nun's.

Jasmine chewed her bottom lip, shaking her head as she set down the last item. "I don't…" She glanced at the bar owner standing a few feet away and leaned closer to Asher. Her warm breath tickled his ear. "Don't let our shifter friend know, but I don't think any of these things belonged to Jean Lafitte."

Asher turned his head slightly toward hers. "None of them?"

"No." She didn't pull away, and if they weren't in the middle of a crowded bar, he might have given in to the temptation to turn all the way until their lips met. To kiss her like he'd wanted to the first time she pressed her lips to his.

Instead, he leaned back slightly, looking into her eyes. "Are you sure?"

She straightened. "Are you doubting me?"

"No. I mean… They pride themselves on being authentic here, so I thought, surely, *something* would have belonged to him."

"I felt his energy when he was on me, stealing mine. It was muddled with a dozen others, but… If they have artifacts that belonged to him, these aren't them." She slid off the stool and waved to Buck. "Thank you. We got what we needed."

The gator shifter nodded as he poured a beer, and Asher followed Jasmine out the door, onto the sidewalk.

The second she saw the mass of spirits hanging out on the streets, she turned on her heel and marched back into the building.

"I tried to be inconspicuous with my protection this time, but it doesn't feel nearly as strong as the skirt." She toyed with the aluminum bracelets on her wrists and glanced down at the circles she wore around her ankles. "Why are so many of them on Bourbon Street?"

He stepped inside. "It's where most of the tourists come when they're alive. I assume the fun and debauchery is attractive to the dead too."

"Let's exit out the back. I know someone who can help." She stopped at the bar on her way to the door. "The hoop skirt I had on yesterday. The one that got caught in the fireplace. Where is it?"

The gator man returned the knife to its display spot on the wall. "I threw that mangled piece of metal in the trash. I don't keep a lost and found."

"Right. Well, thank you for your time. Hopefully we won't be back." She laced the last part with enough venom to stun a grizzly bear. Buck grunted in response.

The back door led into a courtyard shaded by a towering magnolia tree, and they followed the cobblestone path up a side alley and out onto the street. The ghost population was thinner here, but Jasmine strode like a woman on a mission, making a wide berth around the dead.

Asher kept her pace, walking beside her, and what a sight they must have been. They both wore all black, as those who dealt with the dead tended to do, and with his height and pale skin and her jet-black hair and determined expression, they must have looked like a couple of goths on their way to a graveyard.

As they approached an intersection, Jasmine stopped to look both ways, up, down, and around in a circle, the tightness in her jaw and neck indicating she was more concerned with the ghosts than traffic.

"Where are we going?" He followed her across the street and toward a museum.

"To see my sister. If anyone is going to have an authentic Jean Lafitte artifact, it's the history museum, and she just happens to work there."

Jasmine stopped outside the entrance, not so Asher could open the door for her, but to text her sister that she was there. He, however, did not disappoint, not even hesitating when she paused. He opened the door and stood aside, waiting for her to enter before following her in.

Who knew Death had such good manners?

Inside the lobby, he stopped next to her, gently placing a hand on her arm. "How are you feeling? Did your foil protection work, or do you need to rest?"

She moistened her lips, and his gaze dropped to her mouth for at least the third time today. "I'm fine. Thanks for asking." She was definitely not imagining the attraction now...was she? Being near him scrambled her thoughts, so who knew? At this point she couldn't tell her head from a hole in the ground.

"That's good." He smiled, and the pale blue of his irises took on an inner glow briefly before dimming again.

As she stared into his eyes, she found herself drifting closer to him, yearning to close the distance between them, to find out if the kindness and caring he was beginning to display were real. *Not good, Jazz. Snap out of it.*

She cleared her throat. "Um… What about you? Are you doing okay without your connection to the underworld?"

"I've been better, but I'll survive. I hope."

"Me too."

"It's about time you came to see me." Ella strode toward her, stopping to put her hands on her hips. "You were supposed to call me after the bachelorette party. What happened?"

So much. Where did she even begin? "Asher, this is my sister, Ella."

"Asher!" Ella gave Jasmine a conspiratorial wink, though what she thought they were conspiring about, she had no clue. She wasn't exactly discreet about it either. "It's so nice to finally meet you."

Ella took his hand, holding it way longer than necessary for a handshake, which meant she was using her friggin' empath power to read him, after Jasmine had explicitly told her not to.

"Hello." Asher grinned, cutting his gaze between them. "Twins?"

"We are," Ella said. "I am so glad you two made up. Jasmine was just telling me the other night about—"

"Hey, El?" If looks could kill, Jasmine would have been firing an automatic weapon. "A word, please?" She gave Asher an apologetic smile. "Excuse us for a minute." Grabbing her by the arm, she dragged her sister out of his earshot.

"That boy is crazy about you. I guess you won't need to freeze your eggs after all, right?" Ella's smile lit up her whole face. "I'm so happy for you."

"Don't be. We're not together." Though she couldn't

deny the little thrill shimmying up her spine at her sister's assessment.

Ella took a deep breath, gripping her hand and reading her like she'd promised not to. Again. "I don't detect a trace of that H-word you were claiming to feel the other night, and him… Well, he's confused as all get-out, but who isn't when it comes to you? You, dear sister, are an enigma. Why all this concern? He's ripe for the picking."

"First of all, ew. Don't ever say that again. And second… I don't know. I guess I'm still afraid of rejection."

Ella tilted her head and pressed her lips together, clearly seeing right through the walls Jasmine was attempting to rebuild. "Have you talked about the kiss? What was his excuse for running away?" Ella grinned at Asher over Jasmine's shoulder and wiggled her fingers in a wave.

Jasmine snatched her hand down. "We haven't, and we're not going to any time soon. We have a much more pressing problem, and getting emotions involved will only make it harder. So, will you stop with the matchmaking and help us?"

"Oh, all right. I've got to get back to work anyway. What do you need?"

Jasmine called Asher over and explained the escaped pirate and the problems he was causing. "And now that he's absorbed so much energy from other ghosts, and with Asher's door locked, he's having trouble locating him."

Ella blinked. "Wow. That's a…"

"An irresponsible thing to do." Asher shook his head. "I know. It was stupid, and I take full responsibility."

"You were overworked. Everyone needs a break now and then, and how were you to know a soul would use the entrance as an exit?" Jasmine slipped her hand into his.

She had no idea why. It just felt like the thing to do, so she did it. No judging. "It was an honest mistake, and we're going to fix it."

He looked at their joined hands and then into her eyes. The inner glow in his irises flared again as he swallowed, not saying anything, not pulling from her grasp either.

Okay, fine. She knew exactly why she did it. If he really was crazy about her like Ella claimed, it wouldn't hurt to show him he might still have a chance with her.

She squeezed his fingers before letting him go and shooting her sister a pointed look. "We think we can locate him together, but I'll need something that belonged to the ghost in order to find him. Do you think you could snag an artifact for me to hold?"

"Absolutely," Ella said.

Jasmine's breath came out in a rush of relief, and Asher's posture relaxed.

"In about a week." Ella grimaced. "We have several artifacts that belonged to Lafitte, but they're all on loan to the Museum of Tampa History in Florida. They've got a 'Pirates of the Gulf' event going on."

"Satan's balls." Asher clenched his fists at his sides. "It's not safe for you to be…" He clamped his mouth shut.

"It's okay. She knows about the weakness. Our dad is a necromancer too, and you're right. With that many ghosts wandering the streets, it's not safe for any necromancer to be outside unprotected."

Ella raised her brow. "I'm sure you can think of plenty of other things to talk about…to *do*…inside while you wait for the artifact."

Would it be wrong to strangle her sister right here in the museum lobby? Or maybe just backhand her across the face? Asher was fighting a grin, so he obviously knew what Ella was insinuating, and Jasmine could not have been more mortified. Especially since she couldn't stop picturing those *other things* she could do with Asher.

He finally broke the awkward silence, a sly smile lifting one side of his mouth. "Actually, I do have an idea of something we can do in the meantime. Let's go back to your place."

Oh, boy.

CHAPTER ELEVEN

Nausea churned in Jasmine's stomach, her palms slicking with sweat as she looked up into Asher's pale blue eyes. He'd portaled them home to keep her away from the ghost horde—despite the fact the act drained his power every time he did it—and now they stood in her living room, face to face, his expression unreadable.

Well, it might have been readable if she had more experience with the living. It was impossible to read the expression of a reanimated corpse...broken synapses and all...so she was out of practice.

Cameron had made himself scarce since he'd figured out how to operate the handle on the back door with his kitty paws, so here she was, alone with the one man who had the power to either breathe life into her heart or crush it, and he had an "idea" of something they could do while they waited for the artifact. *Holy bed sheets.* Did she have time to put on a clean set?

Was it wise to jump right into this? They hadn't even talked about their feelings for each other. Then again, actions spoke louder than words, and if he was ready for some action, she could certainly turn up the volume. *No. Words first, Jazz.*

"Um...maybe we should talk first if you really wanna do this. I mean, I'm game. It's been a while, but we should probably set up some ground rules before we jump into it." What was she saying? Words were not the way to go. She'd just told her sister getting involved with Asher would complicate their mission, yet here she was offering herself up to him like she was the one ripe for the picking. *Ew. Now I'm saying it.*

"I agree. It's going to be complicated, but I think we can pull it off. I'm used to slipping in and out and delivering the goods, so the hard part lies on you."

Her mouth opened and closed a few times while she attempted to maintain her poise. "It's not like I'm inexperienced." Why did she sound so breathless? *Woman up, Jazz.*

"I know, but I doubt you've been where I'm going to take you." Damn, he had a heart-melting grin.

And wasn't he confident in his prowess? She wasn't sure if the cocky attitude was a turn on or a red flag, but she had to admit the banter was fun. With Ella's observation of Asher's emotions fueling her confidence, Jasmine couldn't wait to follow through. "As I said, I'm not inexperienced. What makes you think you can take me anywhere I haven't been before?"

He pursed his lips, giving her a quizzical look. "You've been to the aether? I thought you couldn't portal."

"Oh, you're talking about the aether." She let out a nervous laugh. A mortified laugh, to be honest because, *holy miscommunication*, this conversation was not headed in the direction she thought it was. "No, yeah, I've never been there."

"What did you think I was talking about?"

She slowly shook her head, trying to regain her composure and drag her mind out of the gutter. "Doesn't matter. Come and sit. Tell me about this plan of yours." She fisted her hand and made a hook motion like a gung-ho pirate. Like an idiot. Who did she think she was? Popeye?

Gesturing to the couch, she watched as Asher sank onto the cushion, his dark jeans hugging his muscular thighs, his black t-shirt contrasting with his fair skin, drawing her eye to his chiseled biceps.

Speaking of Popeye... "Do you eat spinach?" Because he looked like he'd be strong to the finish. *Cut it out, girl. You wanna scare the boy away again?* Just because he liked her, it didn't mean he was going to act on it. She needed to play it cool this time, avoid another incident.

"It's not my favorite, but I sometimes do. Why?"

"No reason." She sat next to him, angling her body to face him, and dammit if her knee didn't brush against his.

He glanced down, not bothering to move away, so she left it there, resting against him like she'd imagined the rest of her body would be doing by now. This was better, though. Knees were safe.

He inhaled deeply, a look of indecision forming in his eyes as he opened his mouth and closed it again. Shaking his head, he rose, pacing in front of the sofa before his gaze locked on a ball of foil in the corner of the room.

"You turned your apartment into a Faraday cage, right? Spirits can't come inside?"

"Yeah. It's not pretty, but it works."

"How does it work?" He stopped pacing and faced her.

"I set up the aluminum around the perimeter, and

then I instilled it with my magic. I have to recharge it every now and then, but it's never failed me."

"Do you think you could make one that keeps ghosts *in* rather than *out*? A Faraday cage that actually acts as a cage instead of a barrier?" His eyes were calculating, his expression all business.

She chewed her bottom lip. "You want me to make a trap for Lafitte?"

"Yes, but more than that. You can't be out in the Quarter searching for him when there are a thousand energy siphons roaming around, waiting to drain you."

"That's true, but I can't stay in here twenty-four-seven, either."

"Right. So, what if you made a cage, and I rounded up the spirits and put them inside it?"

"That many ghosts inside a small space would draw attention. Even the humans would catch on. Being on the Earthly plane is making the spirits crazy."

He started pacing again. "Which is why we'd put them in the aether. I can portal you there, you set up the cage, and then I'll bring you back to this plane. You can hang out while I grab the ghosts and move them to the cage. With the Quarter clear of the dead—or at least as clear as it used to be—you'll get your strength back, and we'll be ready to face Lafitte together."

Jasmine leaned back on the couch, folding her hands in her lap. His idea made sense, and once they caught the pirate, he'd have all his marks in one place, which would make it easier to get them to the underworld and out of her hair for good.

But it was more than that, this plan of his. He needed her help for it to work. He needed *her*. "So we'd be working as a team? Communicating, helping each other?"

He sat next to her, taking her hands in his. "I think we'd make a great team."

Screw it. Emotions were involved whether she wanted them to be or not. It was time they talked about *the incident.* "Then why did you get weird before?"

"I'm sorry. You caught me off guard, and my feelings for you scared the hell out of me." He chuckled. "Almost literally."

"What do you mean?"

He cupped her face in his hand, running his thumb over her cheek. "I mean I screwed up. Leaving like I did, avoiding you, taking your marks with no explanation... I never should have done any of it, and from this point forward, I promise not to shut you out. I don't have a problem with your occupation or your magic, and I'm sorry I let you believe I did. Can you forgive me?"

She closed her eyes, nuzzling into his palm as his words sank in. Asher was death, and death was scared of love. His vulnerability was adorable, and as she looked into his eyes, the pale blue inner glow pulsed, melting her heart.

Smiling, she laced her fingers through his. "I can forgive you, but you're going to have to work for it."

"I'll do whatever it takes." He drifted toward her, gently pressing his lips to hers.

If it were possible for a mortal to die and come back to life, she might as well change her name to Frankenstein's monster, because kissing Asher sent her to heaven and back again. His lips were soft, not quite as warm as a human's, but the kiss packed enough heat to set fire to her heart.

She leaned into him, threading her hands behind his neck and pulling him closer, drinking him in. He tentatively placed a hand on her hip, sliding the other into her hair to cradle the back of her head.

With a shuddering breath, he pressed his forehead to hers, a smile touching his eyes. "I'm sorry I didn't let that happen before. I didn't know what I was missing."

"Hmm." She tried for a witty comeback, but the tingling in her lips and the warmth blooming below her navel were too distracting. They were supposed to be doing something. Solving some kind of problem, but at that moment, she didn't care.

"So…" He brushed his lips to hers, tucking her hair behind her ear before rising to his feet. "About that ghost trap."

She blinked, her senses finally returning. "Yeah. Where?" It seemed she still couldn't form a complete sentence.

"Anywhere, really. It's another dimension, so it shouldn't affect this plane. But it would be nice to put it somewhere that correlates with a secluded spot on Earth, so no one notices us going in and out."

"How about my back courtyard? It's got a brick fence surrounding it."

"Neighbors?"

"All supes."

He grinned. "That's perfect."

Jasmine led Asher to the courtyard, and he helped her move her aluminum fence posts—which were really six-inch rocks wrapped in foil—onto the porch to create an open space for ghosts to enter her property. Placing her hand on one of the relocated balls, she checked for the vibrating energy to register on her skin, signaling her perimeter was still intact, simply smaller.

As she rose to her feet and turned around, she found

Asher grinning like a kid on his birthday. Did reapers have birthdays? Were they even born, or were they magically created? Making a mental note to ask him her laundry list of questions now that they were on kissing—*ahem...* speaking—terms, she rested a hand on her hip. "You look happy."

"The aether is like a sanctuary for reapers. Most of us live there, since reapers crave solitude. It's peaceful." His smile widened. "I'm excited to show it to you."

"I'm excited to see it." And to learn more about this intriguing, multidimensional man. "Why don't you live there?"

He laughed. "I'm an anomaly. I actually like people, which means I can..." He lowered his gaze for a moment. "I can't wait for you to experience it with me. Are you ready?"

Truth be told, the thought of going into another dimension did make her a teensy bit nauseated. Her heart thudded, and the sticky summer heat seemed to intensify. "I'm not going to get stuck there, am I?" She picked up the roll of foil she'd left on the porch, tucking it under her arm.

"No. We portal in and out, no different than going somewhere on the earthly plane." He pulled his pen from his pocket and offered her his hand.

As she slipped her palm into his, he extended his scythe and sliced through the air, creating a gateway to an actual other dimension. She knew it was possible. Hell, she could even locate ghosts and latch onto their energy when they were in the aether; it shouldn't have been so awe-inspiring. But it was.

She peered into the opening, but instead of seeing another colorful scene on Earth, her gaze found gray emptiness. The aether looked like it sat in the middle of a storm cloud, and as Asher stepped through the portal, her pulse kicked into a sprint. She wasn't meant to be in that space. She could feel it in her bones.

But he pulled her through. The minute the gateway closed behind her, she froze. Her warm life energy seeped out through her pores, and cold shivers racked her body. She gasped, throwing on her bubble of protection and gripping Asher's arm. Her magical shield helped, but the sensation of being inside the aether felt an awful lot like when a ghost was drawing her energy.

Perhaps it wasn't the spirits themselves that caused her harm, but their connection to this place that Asher so loved. The air was heavy, and the gravitational pull felt ten times stronger, making her movements sluggish and strained.

"It's nice, isn't it?" He patted her shoulder and took the roll of foil from her hand. "So quiet. When ghosts are here, they just hang out, floating in a sort of semi-conscious state, recharging."

"It's...great." She forced a smile, not about to tell him his sacred place felt like it was sucking the life out of her. "Let's get this cage set up. We need to roll the foil into balls and create a circle with them. Everything feels heavier in here, so I don't think we need to worry about them rolling away."

"Does it feel heavy?" He smiled as he followed her instructions, rolling the foil between his hands.

"A little bit." She arranged the aluminum into a circle and kneeled, resting her hands on two of the balls. Activating her magic, she sent it out through her right hand, connecting it into a solid ring as the vibration reached around the circumference into her left hand. As she stood, her magic flared to life, illuminating the cage in sparkling light.

"Whoa." She stepped back, next to Asher. "It's never done that before."

"That's the magic of the aether mixing with yours. It's beautiful." He rested a hand on the small of her back, and if she didn't feel like she was about to keel over, she might have been thrilled at the intimacy of his touch.

"I'm not sure how you're going to get the ghosts inside, though. It blocks spirit energy from both sides. I had to break the circle around my house to get Cameron inside before I put him in the cat."

"Let's see." He pressed the tip of his scythe into the sparkling energy and drew it downward. The magic parted as if he were slicing through softened butter, reforming when he withdrew his scythe, making the perimeter whole again. "I think that'll work."

"Sounds great." Her toes were going numb, and her head spun. "Do you mind taking me home? I don't want to tempt fate."

"I suppose it's a lot to take in, isn't it? Thank you for sharing this with me. I've never brought anyone in here before."

"It was an experience, for sure." She pretended to grab an imaginary scythe and made a slicing motion. "Thanks for bringing me." She'd mull over the significance of being his first—was this the equivalent of meeting his parents?—later, when she could feel her feet again.

Asher opened a portal, and Jasmine didn't hesitate. She jumped through, landing on her porch and sucking in the biggest breath she'd ever taken. *Suffocating spirits.* The aether wasn't made for mortals. She'd have to be dead before she ever ventured into that life-sucking void again. The aether would kill her.

Her toes were still numb, no doubt from lack of blood flow since her heart had been working overtime to keep her lungs alive. She dropped onto the couch and leaned her head back, closing her eyes as Asher sank down next to her.

"Are you okay?" His fingers grazed her jawline, and she shivered.

"I'm fine. Creating the cage was a drain on my energy. Nothing a little rest won't fix." That wasn't entirely a lie. Supernatural Faraday cages weren't easy to make, but this level of fatigue had come from that awful place. "What's the plan?"

He pressed his lips to her forehead. "Why don't you have a nap, and I'll see how many ghosts I can round up before you wake?"

"Okay." He'd get no argument from her on that front. She was spent. Lying back, she rested her head on a pillow, and Asher took the afghan from an armchair, draping it over her. "Feel free to portal in whenever you're done. No need to knock."

He leaned down to kiss her, but his lips had barely brushed hers when Cameron leaped onto the arm of the couch.

"What did I miss? Apparently, a lot."

CHAPTER TWELVE

"You've been dead for two weeks, Julia. It's time to start the process of crossing over." Asher caught the spirit in the crook of his scythe and carried her into the aether faster than a human could blink.

"I'm not dead. What is this place?" She jerked her head around frantically, searching the emptiness. "Who are you?"

"I'm Death, come to take you home."

"Are you serious?" Her voice cracked.

"Dead serious." Asher pleaded with his eyes, despite the throbbing headache in his temple. Her defiance of her fate drew on his energy, not to the extent the spirits affected Jasmine, but with his power source cut off behind his locked door, too many stubborn ghosts could be detrimental.

Panic tightened her eyes, but she shook her head, still resisting. "What are you really? One of those vampire weirdos who actually thinks they're a creature of the night? Or are you just some loser who never outgrew his teenage goth phase?"

Asher's nostrils flared as he sucked in a breath. He didn't have the time or the energy for this. "I told you, I'm Death."

Calling on his magic, he morphed into his reaper form, his face turning skeletal, blue flames igniting in his eye sockets as he towered over the impudent woman.

She opened her mouth as if to scream, but no sound was emitted. Her eyes widened, a look of sheer terror contorting her features as the ash gray of her pallor turned white, and she lifted her trembling hands to her face. "I'm dead?" she squeaked.

If he could have rolled his eyes, he would have, but since he didn't have actual eyeballs in this form, he simply shook his head. "That's what I've been trying to tell you. Let's go." He yanked her through the aether, briefly landing in Jasmine's back yard before opening another gateway to their ghost trap and locking the woman inside.

Slipping back into his human form and onto the earthly plane, he trudged up the porch and stepped into Jasmine's kitchen. She sat at the table, sipping a glass of iced tea and looking much better than he felt.

"Nice nap?" He sank into a chair and took a sip from the glass she offered him. Refreshing and sweet, the tea slid down his throat, cooling him from the inside out. "You look better. Radiant, actually."

Her cheeks reddened as she wiped the condensation from the side of her glass. "I don't know about radiant, but I feel better. How's the ghost round-up going?"

"Slow." He set his glass down, resting his hand on the table. "The ones who are willing are easy, but the stubborn ones... I never realized they suck my energy too until my power supply was cut off. It doesn't help that I have to chase them down. I can't call them to me like you can. At this rate, you're going to be stuck inside until your sister comes through with that Lafitte artifact. I suppose I can portal you to work, but even doing that is starting to give me a headache."

"Don't worry about my job. I called them and took some vacation days, so I can help you."

"Vacation." He sank lower in his chair, a heaviness forming in his chest. "I'm sorry. I don't know why I thought I could get away with that." Or why he thought it would help.

"No." She placed her hand on top of his. "I never knew how hard you worked. I don't blame you for wanting some time off. Everyone needs a break."

All he'd needed was to come to terms with his fate, and none of this would have happened. He hadn't needed a break. He'd needed to make Jasmine his. He laced his fingers through hers. All wasn't lost yet. "Reapers don't. We're born to reap souls."

"So you *were* born." The corners of her mouth tugged upward. "I wondered where you came from."

He laughed. "Did you think I was magically formed in the bowels of hell?"

"I considered the possibility." She shrugged, gazing into his eyes like she was looking inside him, seeing him for what he truly was. *Almost.*

Heat crept up his neck. "And it didn't bother you?"

"Should it have?"

He took her other hand across the table. "I think it would terrify most people."

"I'm not most people."

"You are definitely not." She was passionate, strong, beautiful, and not the slightest bit scared of him. Well, not scared of him in human form anyway, but it was a start.

She brought out a side of him he didn't know existed, made him feel things he didn't think possible. Things that shouldn't have been possible if he were a normal reaper.

She glanced at their joined hands before returning her gaze to his eyes. "I'm sorry I hated you."

"I'm sorry I made you hate me." He rubbed his thumb across the back of her hand. "Where's Cameron?"

"Sleeping on the back porch. He's still not used to the intricacies of being a cat. I caught him licking himself below the belt, and now he's mortified. Swears he didn't realize he was doing it."

Asher laughed. "I mean, if I could lick myself below the belt…"

"Who wouldn't, right?" Her smile touched her eyes, and he lost himself in her gaze.

"Can I tell you something about me? Something most people don't know?"

She arched a brow. "You know my secret weakness. It's only fair I know something about you."

His heart beat so fast you could have heard it knocking against his chest, and his mouth went dry as a small Texas town on a Sunday afternoon. He took a gulp of tea, wiping his sweaty palms on his jeans before taking her hands again. "Normal reapers aren't capable of experiencing romantic emotions—giving or receiving them."

Wariness tightened her eyes. "Then how are new reapers conceived? Is it just wham, bam, thank you ma'am, and you've got a new baby Death running around? I don't…" Shaking her head, she pulled from his grasp. "I don't understand what you're trying to tell me. Are you saying what's happening between us isn't…"

He stood, tugging her to her feet. "I'm not a normal reaper, Jasmine. You know that."

"Okay…"

Hell's bells, this wasn't coming out right. *Just tell the woman how you feel, dammit.* "I'm trying to say I have romantic feelings for you." As he put his hands on her hips, her eyes softened. "I always have."

She rested her hands on his shoulders. "Well, don't I feel special? I caught the eye of a man who's not supposed to have an eye for me to catch."

"You are very special."

Lacing her fingers behind his neck, she tilted her head. "What were you so scared of, then? If you've always had romantic feelings for me, why the dramatic exit when I kissed you?"

He'd been dancing around that questions for days. Should he tell her the truth? Admit everything that could happen if they fell in love? That their fates would be tied, the expectations for them to have a family? What if she didn't want children?

He couldn't. It was too much too soon, and it might not even matter if they couldn't find the damn pirate before his magic ran out. "I guess I wasn't expecting you to have feelings for me too. I'm a symbol of death."

"And I'm a necromancer. Duh. I like you, Asher. I always have, even when I hated you." Rising onto her toes, she pressed her warm, soft lips to his.

Never in his life had he felt anything like the elation her admission produced. It was like that kitten poster hanging on his wall all these years was telling him to "hang in there" for this precise moment.

He slid his arms around her waist, holding her close and memorizing the way her body felt pressed against his. A gentle moan escaped her throat, making heat pool in his groin, and he reached for the doorknob, twisting the lock.

He'd hung in there long enough. He needed this woman like hell needed the souls of the damned.

Unhooking her fingers from behind his neck, she slid her hands down his chest, slipping them under his shirt, the warmth of her skin raising goosebumps on his flesh. She lifted the fabric, and he helped by yanking it over his head.

His core tightened at her gasp, and her gaze blazed a trail of heat down his stomach, her tongue slipping out to moisten her lips as her eyes locked on the bulge in his jeans.

"May I?" He gently gripped the hem of her shirt, and she raised her arms, allowing him to lift it over her head and lay it on the counter.

She wore a simple, black satin bra, understated, yet so Devil-damned sexy he couldn't help but grunt his approval. This woman had awakened something primal inside him. A need so great it consumed his soul.

"You are so beautiful, Jasmine." He took her in his arms, kissing her passionately before trailing his lips along her jaw and down her neck, reveling in the way her skin turned to gooseflesh beneath his touch.

After unhooking her bra, he tossed it aside before sweeping her into his arms and carrying her to the living room. As he laid her on the couch, she wiggled out of the rest of her clothes, a naked goddess gazing up at him, beckoning him with a devilish smile.

He could have stood there staring at her all afternoon, marveling at her beauty, but the longing in her eyes called to him, silently begging him to touch her, to please her. How could he resist?

He removed the rest of his clothes and kneeled beside her, running his hands along her curves, trailing his lips across her soft skin. Her nipples hardened into pearls beneath his tongue. Her body responded to his caresses as if he were made with the sole purpose of pleasing her.

Kissing his way down her stomach, he found her sweet spot, circling her sensitive nub with his tongue until she cried out, her hips bucking as she gasped for air. As her breathing slowed, he climbed on top of her, settling between her legs. He teased her opening with his tip as he kissed her neck, letting the anticipation build until he was hotter than hell itself.

Jasmine clutched his shoulders, her voice thick with need. "You already rang the bell. The door is wide open."

He pushed inside her, his body shuddering as she enveloped him. They fit together perfectly, like they were made for each other, and he slid his arms beneath her, holding her tight as he began to move.

She moaned, the sound so erotic he lost himself in the moment. They were the only two people in the world, and now they were one. How did he ever believe he could exist without this woman?

Her hips moved in time with his thrusts, and as she cried his name again, he found his release. Stars danced around the edges of his vision, his blood humming with ecstasy. As a creature from hell, he had never dreamed he'd experience heaven, but he'd wager this was pretty damn close.

CHAPTER THIRTEEN

"I guess I should get back to work." Asher propped his head on his hand. "Those ghosts aren't going to vanquish themselves." He and Jasmine lay on their sides, front to front on her sofa, his hand resting on the curve of her hip.

As a being from hell, he didn't create much body heat on his own—they didn't need it in the sweltering under-world—so lying here with Jasmine felt like he was wrapped in an electric blanket...both his body and soul.

She looked at him, her tongue slipping out to moisten her lips, and he nearly said to hell with it all and carried her to the bedroom to make love to her again. But there would be time for that later, when he was sure she'd be safe stepping outside of her home.

She traced a finger along his lower lip, and her smile made his heart race all over again. "How about I help you?"

He unwedged himself from between her body and the back of the couch, immediately missing her warmth as he sat up. "It's too dangerous for you on the streets right now."

"Who says I have to go on the streets?" She sat next to him, draping her legs across his lap. "You can't call the spirits to you, but I can. I'll stand in the back yard and lasso some ghosts, and you can put them in the cage. It'll be like a supernatural calf scramble at the rodeo."

He glided his fingers along her shins. Being close to her felt so...right. "I thought you needed something that belonged to the ghost to summon it." Did she have any idea the effect she had on him? It was all he could do to stop himself from tossing her on her back and taking her right then and there.

Laughing, she moved her leg, allowing his dick to spring to attention again. Yep, she knew.

"If you want someone specific, I do. Spirit energy all feels the same unless I can pick up specific nuances that are left behind in an object. I won't be able to tell you which ones should go and which are supposed to stay on Earth, but I can grab them, even command the ones that get ornery and refuse to cross over." She stood and collected their clothes, tossing his pants to him. "It'll go much faster if I help."

Having her help would make the job go twice as quickly, if not more, but... "Can you make yourself another one of those steampunk dresses? You know, to protect yourself?"

She gave him a sly look as she buttoned her shorts. "For my protection, or because it makes me look hot?"

He laughed. "Both."

"You got it."

She made another dress, and damn did she look good. Not just because of the steampunk vibe—which had always pushed the right buttons for him—but because she wasn't the slightest bit embarrassed or ashamed to be seen in public with it on. She didn't care what other people thought; she simply did what she had to do. She was tenacious, focused, and oh so sexy.

He was falling for her hard.

They spent the rest of the week working together, Jasmine reaching out with her necromancy magic and nabbing the spirits while Asher escorted them to the aether and locked them in the magical cage. She steered clear of the portals when he opened them, apparently not finding the silent emptiness of the aether as appealing as he did.

That was fine. He and Jasmine went together like salt and chocolate—an unlikely combination that turned out to be sheer perfection when combined. Reaping souls was a solitary business. He'd never experienced the benefits and...dare he say it...*fun* of teamwork. Spending time with Jasmine felt like he was finally home.

While they worked most of the day—wrangling spirits was a hard job—they took breaks to eat and rest, getting to know each other. Asher fell harder and harder with each bad joke she cracked.

By the end of each day they were both exhausted, so every night he left Cameron to watch over her while she recovered, and he slipped into the aether to recharge on the remnants of his magic still floating in the void.

In the mornings, he'd return to find her cooking breakfast, a soft smile on her lips as she kissed him hello. Nothing in his entire existence had ever felt so right. He wanted to spend the rest of his life with her, even if that meant his life would have an end—a revelation he now accepted easily. He'd never truly lived until now.

With Jasmine's help, he had the ghostly Faraday cage filled to the brim, and while the spirits relaxed in the aether, going into an almost catatonic state and no longer trying to consume each other, the strain on the cage became evident when body parts started bulging out the sides like a popped-open can of biscuits. He did his best to shove them back in, but it was like trying to stuff a sleeping bag back into its roll after camping. They never fully fit, no matter how hard he tried.

As he sliced an opening into the cage and tried to work a particularly grouchy man inside, the spirit slipped from Asher's grasp. The ghost bolted, trying to escape, but Asher caught him with his scythe, holding him until the calming effects of the aether subdued him.

This wasn't going to work. There were too many ghosts and not enough cage. Jasmine had mentioned that she occasionally had to recharge the perimeter around her house, so maybe that was all it needed. He opened a portal to her back yard and poked his head through. "Hey, beautiful."

"All done in there?" She backed up, her hands curling into fists.

"I think I need your help. The cage is full, and it's starting to leak."

She moved up onto the porch. "I'm picturing slimy green ectoplasm pooling on the floor, so could you be a little more specific?"

"Imagine the Pillsbury Dough Boy in a corset that won't lace all the way up."

She cringed. "It's about to explode like the Stay Puft Marshmallow Man."

"Do you think you can come in here and recharge it?

Maybe bring another roll of foil so we can make it bigger?"

She chewed her bottom lip, splaying her fingers before fisting her hands again. "Yeah. I can do that. Hold on."

After disappearing into the house, she returned with a roll of foil and stopped outside the portal. With a deep inhale and a nod of resolution, she leaned forward, lifting one leg as if preparing to take a step, but she put her foot down. "I can't."

"Don't worry. I'll be here the whole time. Or..." He paused as the realization formed in his mind. "Does the aether make you sick?" Why hadn't he thought of that possibility before?

"It's not that. I physically can't cross through. Look." She tried again to take a step but seemed to be blocked by an invisible wall.

"It's probably your dress. The energy in here is different, more like that of a ghost." A ghost. *Satan's balls.* It was the aether that zapped her energy, not the process of creating the cage. "Never mind. I'll figure something out."

But she'd already unhooked her suspenders, dropping the hoopskirt to the ground and stepping through the entrance before he could finish his sentence.

"Here." She tossed him the foil, and instinct forced him to catch it, letting the portal close behind him. "Make some balls so we can extend this, while I recharge the magic."

"Jasmine." He caught her wrist. "You can't be in here. It's this place that's hurting you."

"I know." She tugged from his grasp and kneeled beside the cage, hovering her hand above one of the foil balls.

"You need to go." He gripped her bicep, tugging her to

her feet. They were so close. The Lafitte artifact was scheduled to return to the museum tomorrow, and then they could find the culpable pirate and end this fiasco for good. "This was supposed to be a temporary fix to keep you safe. You're not safe here."

"And if all these ghosts escape into my backyard, I won't be safe in my home either. I built that perimeter to keep out the occasional wandering spirit. It won't hold against five hundred at once, so let me do this, please."

"Jasmine."

"We can stand here arguing about it, but eventually you'll have to put me in there with the rest of the ghosts if we do. I can't feel my toes, so start making those balls before I go from tired to dead tired."

Asher nodded and jerked a length of foil from the roll, frantically rolling the balls and letting them drop at his feet while Jasmine reinforced the existing walls. All she had to do was touch a piece of foil, and the bulging around it contracted.

Well, she was probably doing more than touching it—he had no idea how her magic worked—but her power amazed him. The extra boost didn't last long though, and the sides began to bulge again like an overinflated balloon.

"I'm going to move these balls back one at a time and slide in a new one. For a second or two, there'll be a gap in the perimeter, so I'll need you to stand guard."

"Got it." Asher gripped his scythe in both hands, ready to swat the ghosts back into the cage.

The moment Jasmine moved a ball, the grumpy man darted out, and Asher caught him around the waist with his scythe. The ghost struggled, but he dragged him back to the cage, shoving him inside as Jasmine reconnected the magical charge, securing the walls.

"The aether usually subdues them. I've never seen a ghost get that ornery after being in here for a while."

Jasmine rested a hand on the ground and rubbed her forehead. "I think he sucked the crankiness from me on his way out." She shook her head as if shaking off the fact that her life energy was not-so-slowly being drained. "Next." She reached for another ball.

"You need to get out of here."

"Next." She extended the circle again.

Asher stood behind her, catching the escapees and doing his best to block the spirits from draining her further. But the simple act of being inside this dimension was turning out to be deadly.

Her movements grew more and more sluggish, her breathing labored as she crawled around the circle, extending the border and instilling it with what little magic she had left.

"Please, Jasmine. I can handle it now. You need to go home."

On her hands and knees, she looked over her shoulder. "I'm almost done, and I'm going to finish it. Are we clear?"

He kneeled beside her. "Transparent."

"Good."

"No, I mean you're turning transparent. Look at your legs." Taking her by the shoulders, he helped her into a sitting position with her legs stretched out in front of her. Not only had the skin up to her knees turned ashy gray, but he could see through it.

She wiggled her feet, running her hands along her shins. "Well, that can't be good."

"You need to come with me if you want to live." Picking up his scythe, he opened a gateway to her back yard and scooped her into his arms, carrying her through.

He expected her to protest, but instead, she giggled. "I bet I'm the only person in existence who can say they've heard that phrase from a reaper. 'Come with me if you want to live.'" She deepened her voice to mimic him. Then, with a shuddering breath, she held on to his neck and lay her head on his shoulder as he took her inside to her bedroom.

"Is everything okay?" Cameron jumped down from his place on the couch and followed them down the hall.

"She's not well." Asher lay her in bed and unlaced her boots.

"I could have finished expanding the circle." Her eyes fluttered open, and the pressure in Asher's chest eased. At least she still had the strength to be her stubborn self.

As he set her boots on the floor and slipped off her socks, Cameron leaped onto the bed and hissed.

Jasmine glared at the cat. "What's your problem?"

Cameron looked from Jasmine to Asher and back again. "I don't know how to tell you this, but your legs are missing."

"Missing?" She rose onto her elbows, squeezing her eyes shut for a moment before opening them again. "They're a little gray, but they aren't missing. See?" She rotated her feet like windshield wipers.

"What am I supposed to see?" Cameron batted a paw at her leg, but it passed right through her.

Asher's stomach sank. The aether wasn't just draining Jasmine's magic. It was killing her.

"Why? What? Oh, god." Jasmine lay back, covering her face with her hands. "That's why my feet went numb. I'm turning into a ghost."

Asher sat on the edge of the bed, resting a hand on the gray part of her leg. It felt cold and metallic, the same way a spirit felt to his touch when he carried them across to the underworld. "Can you feel my hand?"

"I feel pressure. No warmth. Not that you're all that warm to begin with, but you know what I mean."

He ground his teeth, nodding. With a deep inhale, he reeled in his magic, pulling his inborn ability to touch the dead out of his hand, allowing it to pass through her ghostly leg and lay on the blanket.

She gasped, her eyes going wide, and for the first time since he'd known this incredible woman, he saw fear in her expression. Pulling his hand away, he scooted closer to her face and kissed her forehead.

"No more aether for you."

"I hear you loud and clear. As clear as I hope to ever be." She took his hand, bringing it to her face. "Ella should have the artifact for us tomorrow. Let me rest tonight, and tomorrow we'll end this."

He shook his head. "You're not ending anything. I'll finish it on my own."

"No, Asher. We're in this together. I want to help." The gray on her shins crept up to her knees.

He smiled sadly, his heart wrenching as he brushed the hair away from her face. "I can't lose you, Jasmine. You're the best thing that's ever happened to me."

She smiled. "Are you sure you're not just saying that because I'm one-quarter dead?"

"I'm one hundred percent positive."

Her grip on his hand loosened, her eyelids fluttering like she couldn't keep them open.

"I'll let you get some rest." He kissed her forehead, and she clung to him, gripping his shoulder.

"Stay with me? I don't want to be alone."

"Of course." Asher kicked off his shoes and lay next to her, wrapping his arms around her waist. Her skin was cool to the touch, her legs growing more translucent by the minute. At this rate, she'd be a ghost within the hour.

He refused to let that happen. "Hey, Cameron, would you give us some privacy?"

The cat rose to his paws. "Is she going to be okay?"

Asher stilled, listening to her quiet breaths. "I'll make sure she is."

"All right. I was going to head out to the Garden District and see if I can find my girlfriend, but if you need me..."

"I've got this."

The cat nodded once and leaped from the bed, darting out of the room.

Propping his head on his hand, Asher gazed at Jasmine's peaceful face. The gray on her legs still crept upward. It would take more than a night of rest to stop it from consuming her entire body. She needed magic that was unhindered by the aether. *His* magic.

He placed his hand over her heart, closing his eyes and swallowing hard, praying to whatever gods might be listening that his weakened power would be enough.

He loved her. Of that, he had no doubt. He'd already made up his mind to cut his life short in exchange for a few decades of happiness with her. Once he did this, there would be no turning back.

He didn't *want* to turn back. Ever.

Opening himself up, he called on the magic deep in his soul and sent it into Jasmine, filling her with his essence, tying his fate to hers. As his power coursed through her veins, the color returned to her legs, slowly spreading from her hips down to her feet.

He'd given her a piece of himself, relinquishing his immortality so that she might live.

His lids grew heavy, and he indulged himself, basking in her sweet honeysuckle scent and the warmth of her renewed body pressed into his. But he didn't deserve this respite. This was his problem. He'd created it all by himself, and that's how he should have been solving it. He never should have involved Jasmine, and finding that pirate on his own was the only way to keep her safe.

He closed his eyes for a moment. A quick cat nap would help restore his strength. He'd allow himself twenty minutes of rest, and then he'd bag and tag Lafitte, open his door, and clear New Orleans of all its ghosts so Jasmine could heal.

CHAPTER FOURTEEN

J asmine rolled onto her side and opened her eyes, a smile tugging on her lips as her gaze focused on the sleeping reaper. Blond lashes fringed his closed lids, and the worry lines creasing his forehead had smoothed, making him look serene, almost celestial.

He was angelic in a way, she supposed. An angel of Death. *Her* angel. Her smile widened, her heart kicking into a sprint as she memorized his masculine features. His sharp jawline, his strong cheekbones, the lock of blond hair curling down onto his forehead.

Damn, she had it bad for this man. She always had, if she were honest with herself.

She brushed the hair from his face and rose onto her elbow, but he didn't stir. He must've been just as worn out as she was…though *he* wasn't turning into a ghost.

The blankets still followed the contours of her feet, but she hesitated to pull them back and look. If sleep didn't bring the color back to her skin, she'd be stuck that way. Forced to wear pants in the sweltering heat of summer to hide her invisible legs. Talk about a bad case of swamp ass.

Her toes still had a pins-and-needles sensation, which she could probably ignore, but her screaming bladder demanded attention. With a deep inhale, she closed her eyes and slid her legs out from under the covers. She lifted one lid, then the other, her breath coming out in a whoosh of relief as she took in the light brown color of her skin. She was completely opaque too, aside from her toes, which still looked ghostly gray.

Resting her feet on the floor, she stood and waited, expecting a wave of dizziness to knock her over, but it didn't. Not only was she on the mend, but a hot-as-sin reaper lay sleeping in her bed. Not a bad start to the day.

After a quick visit to the bathroom, she retrieved her phone from the coffee table, excitement bubbling in her chest as she read her sister's text. Ella had slipped a dagger that belonged to Jean Lafitte into her bag at the museum, and she planned to drop it by in two hours.

"Cameron?" she whispered. "Are you here?"

When the cat didn't answer, she grinned and locked the back door. She was alone with Asher for the next two hours. She might as well take advantage of it before they went ghost hunting again.

She padded to her room and found her reaper sitting on the edge of the bed, wringing his hands. He looked up when she entered, his gaze dropping to her legs before his shoulders slumped in relief.

"Thank the Devil it worked."

She rocked back on her heels as she glanced down at her feet. "I told you all I needed was some sleep. It's a weakness, not a fatal flaw."

He made a noncommittal sound in his throat, his brow furrowing as he lowered his gaze.

She moved toward him, resting her hands on his shoulders. "I'm glad you stayed."

"I didn't mean to fall asleep."

"It's better than you lying there staring at me for hours. That would be creepy."

He chuckled and shook his head. "I had big plans to run out while you were sleeping and find Lafitte on my own. I thought with most of the ghosts corralled in your cage, I might be able to recognize his energy now."

"Then you'll be happy to know that Ella is bringing an artifact over in a couple of hours. I'm sure with our magic combined, we'll find him and nab him in no time."

He shook his head. "I need to do this alone. I can't risk losing you."

She pursed her lips. "Don't get all alpha male on me now, mister. We're a team. We'll do it together...after we do something else."

"There's too much at stake. You need to understand—"

She gently pushed him onto his back and leaned over him. "No, *you* need to understand. I'm not now, and I never will be, a damsel in distress. Nothing scares me, and I never back down from a fight."

His eyes glowed dimly, the blue flames dancing in his irises mesmerizing her, pulling her in. She lowered her mouth to his, kissing him passionately before straightening and tugging her shirt over her head.

"I'm also in love with you. Can you handle that?" She unhooked her bra and let it drop to the floor.

Asher swallowed hard, scooting to the center of the mattress before pulling off his shirt. "I believe I can. I'm in love with you too."

"Do you mean that?" She shimmied out of her shorts and crawled onto the bed.

"Every word." He sat up to take her in his arms, but she pushed him onto his back again, straddling his groin.

She lay on top of him, skin to skin, trailing kisses down his neck, across his collarbone, and up to his earlobe, where she nipped the delicate flesh, reveling in his sharp intake of breath and the feel of his strong arms wrapped around her.

His skin was soft and smooth, and his breathing grew shallow as she glided her lips down his chest, toward his stomach. Asher was pure, raw, untamed power. A reaper of souls, able to cross dimensions with a swing of his scythe, yet he yielded to her. His muscles tightened as she neared the waistband of his jeans, and when she palmed his growing arousal, curling her fingers around it through the fabric, he moaned.

Turning her head, she lay her cheek on his stomach as she unbuttoned his pants. His fingers glided through her hair, raising goosebumps on her skin, and she couldn't help herself. She needed a peek at this immortal creature's soul.

Using only her mind and her magic, she reached into his core, running metaphysical fingers over his essence. He gasped and then let out a pleasurable groan, the sound melting in her ears like milk chocolate.

"Careful in there, darling. You might not like what you find."

She closed her eyes, and an image of his reaper form flashed through her mind. A skeletal figure with blue flames for eyes looked into hers, and her heart swelled. Death looked good on him. His energy wrapped around her, buzzing along her bare skin, a strange familiarity registering in her soul. Asher felt like home.

"What do you see?" He stroked her cheek with the backs of his fingers.

"It's more of a feeling." She turned her head, pressing a kiss to his stomach.

"What do you feel?"

"I love you," she whispered against his flesh.

"And I love you."

With a shuddering inhale, she pulled back her magic and looked at him with wonder. His unearthly fair skin had a pink undertone, full of life, and the sinew beneath revealed lean, defined strength. As her gaze met his, the soft blue glow in his eyes sent a shiver down her spine, and he looked at her with a need that said he wanted to consume her.

She was ready to be devoured.

Rising onto her knees, she removed the rest of his clothes, then her own, and he joined her kneeling, gliding the tips of his fingers along her arms before tangling them in her hair and kissing her like he was dying, and she was the only cure.

He flipped her onto her back, the length of his naked body resting against her side, his dick, long and hard, pressing into her hip as his hand roamed over her flesh, teasing her nipples, turning her skin to gooseflesh.

He touched her like he wanted her. Needed her. Though he knew everything about her morbid job and her rare ability, he showered her with affection. And when his fingers found her center, lord have mercy, he showed her the true meaning of need.

"Take me, Asher."

"With pleasure." He settled on top of her, pressing his

tip against her entrance, hesitating. He looked like he might have wanted to say something, but at that point... with *his* point knocking at the door...she couldn't be bothered with words.

Gripping his butt, she lifted her hips, pulling him toward her, inside her. A masculine groan rumbled in his chest as he filled her, and she could have sworn she heard angels singing. He was thick and long, and *holy hellhounds*, she could have died a happy woman at that moment.

He slid out slightly, and an electrical sensation tingled through her core, making her gasp. His gaze met hers, and he smiled, moving his hips in a slow, delicious motion that she savored more than Sweet Destiny's devil's food cake.

But the savoring didn't last long. As his rhythm quickened, pressure built in her abdomen, ecstasy coiling in her core until it unleashed in a tidal wave of elation, exploding outward to the tips of her toes, consuming her in its wake.

Asher stilled, pressing into her as he rode the wave of his own release, and then he relaxed on top of her, nuzzling into her hair. "You are incredible," he growled into her ear, making her shiver.

She grinned, running her fingers along his back before dropping her arms on the mattress. "Meh. I've had better."

He jerked his head up, looking at her quizzically, and she laughed.

"I'm kidding." She cupped his face in her hands. "Asher, you are... I don't even have words for how I feel about you, and you know I always have words."

He smiled and pressed a gentle kiss to her lips. "I've left you speechless."

"Well, I don't know about speechless. I mean the sex was amazing, and when you let me reach into your being like that... You showed me trust, something most people don't have for a woman who reanimates corpses for a living."

He furrowed his brow, a look of conviction in his eyes. "I do trust you."

"I trust you too."

———

Asher lay there, holding Jasmine, basking in the afterglow of making love to the woman of his dreams. To his soulmate. He belonged to her now, whether she could accept his true form or not. If she ever saw him, and she rejected him, it all would have been for nothing.

No, not nothing. He'd had no choice but to join his essence with hers. She wouldn't have survived otherwise. At least, his mind had convinced him she wouldn't at the time. Could she have recovered with sleep like she insisted? Did he bind his fate to hers prematurely? No, not at the rate she was turning ghost.

It didn't matter now anyway. He did it, and now he had to live with the consequences. The world was a better place with Jasmine in it, whether she wanted to be his or not. And after the way they just made love, she seemed willing.

Her peek into his soul had terrified him. If she'd seen what he truly was, she'd have shoved him out of her bed faster than a tourist gets drunk on Bourbon Street during Mardi Gras. Lucky for him, she apparently didn't get any visuals. It probably would have scarred her for life.

He'd made that mistake once. A banshee he'd dated casually a hundred or so years ago had convinced him to show her his true form—his self that only those about to cross over into the underworld got to see. She'd turned whiter than an albino ghost and run away screaming like…well, like a banshee. He never saw her again, though he heard she experienced nightmares for the next three years.

No, he could never let Jasmine see his true form. For her sake and for his.

She rose onto her elbow and traced a finger over his chest. "My sister will be here in an hour."

He closed his eyes, inhaling her sweet floral scent. "I suppose we should get dressed then."

With a sleepy smile, she sat up, the covers falling away from her, exposing her delicious curves and smooth, mouthwatering skin. Her long, dark hair fell over her shoulders, and she brushed it back. "I'm going to take a shower. I'd ask you to join me, but the things I'd want to do to you would take longer than we have."

Warmth bloomed in his groin at her words, and though he wanted to pull her back to the bed and make love to her all over again, he sat up. "I should pop home and do the same. Change my clothes."

She lowered her gaze. "Good idea. Because that tent you're pitching is incredibly distracting."

He followed her gaze to his lap, and sure enough, he'd made a teepee of her sheets. "That's the effect you have on me."

"So it seems. Now get out of here, or we'll never be ready in time. Be back in half an hour, ready to kick some pirate booty."

He laughed and gathered his clothes. "Yes, ma'am."

Asher portaled home, took a quick shower, dressed, and stopped to examine his reflection in the mirror. After giving Jasmine so much of his energy last night, he expected to feel drained. Weak. But he felt the opposite, stronger than he'd felt since this whole fiasco began.

His cheeks held a pink flush, but he wasn't sure if it was his new semi-mortal state or love making his blood hum. Either way, it was a look he'd like to get used to. Now he just had to keep Jasmine alive.

There was no way in all of hell he was letting her get near Lafitte or the aether again.

He portaled back to her living room, and as he stepped inside, he found her sitting on the sofa, chewing her bottom lip and wringing her hands. Her hair was still damp from her shower, and she wore black leggings with a sleeveless onyx shirt. She looked up at him as he moved toward her, and the pain in her dark eyes nearly tore him in two.

"What's wrong?" He sat beside her, taking her hands in his.

She shook her head, refusing to make eye contact. "It's nothing."

"Hey." He gently hooked a finger under her chin, turning her face toward his. "Whatever it is, you can tell me."

She hesitated, her eyes tightening as she studied his. "How old are you?"

He glanced at the ceiling, trying to recall. "Two-hundred-something. I've lost count."

"The average lifespan of an American woman is seventy-eight years." She inhaled a shaky breath and blew it out hard. "I've only got about fifty left."

"Okay?"

"You're immortal, Asher, and I'm going to die. I should've…" She shook her head. "I should have thought about this before I fell in love with you, but you're going to watch me grow old and wrinkly and eventually die. You'll escort me to my fate in the underworld, and then what? You'll move on to the next necromancer?"

"Come here." He pulled her into his arms, holding her tight. "You don't have to worry about that."

"No? Do you have the power to grant me immortality, then?"

"No, I don't. But there's something you should know about reapers." He gripped her shoulders, leaning back to look into her eyes. "When a reaper gives his heart to a necromancer, he gives up part of his immortality."

"Part of it?"

"As long as the necromancer is alive, the reaper maintains his semi-immortal state. He keeps his magic and continues to reap souls, but once his necromancer passes on, the reaper's soul follows her to the underworld."

"I don't understand."

He took her hand in his. "We'll grow old together, and when you die, I'll die too."

Her eyes widened, her mouth gaping for a moment before she spoke, "That's not *part* of your immortality. That's all of it. You can't give up your life for me. I won't let you."

"It's too late. I already have."

"Well, take it back." She slid from his grasp, wrapping her arms around herself. "You're supposed to live forever. I can't... I can't be the reason you die. I mean, fifty years? That's a blink of an eye for someone like you."

"I can't take it back, Jasmine. I've already done it, and anyway, I'd rather spend the next fifty years with you and die a happy man than live the rest of eternity without you."

The muscles in her neck tightened as she ground her

teeth. "What do you mean you've already done it? I didn't agree to anything. We're not married. This kind of thing is a joint venture."

He lifted his hands, dropping them into his lap. "You were dying. I did it to save your life."

"When? Last night? I was fine." She waved her hand like what happened to her was no big deal.

"No, Jasmine. After you asked me to stay, you passed out. The color continued to drain from your legs. You were transparent up to your hips, and it wasn't showing any signs of stopping."

"I…" Her mouth fell open.

"Did you really think a night of sleep was all you needed? You were turning into a ghost. The aether and all the spirits there were killing you, so I did the only thing I could think of. I gave myself to you. I instilled some of my essence inside you, tying my fate to yours. My energy isn't affected by the aether like yours, so it revived you. I gave you as much as I could, and then I held you all night, praying to every god in existence to save you."

"Well…" Her lower lip trembled. "It worked."

"Yes, it did."

"And that's it? We're bound now? I don't get a choice?"

"Of course you get a choice. You can reject me. Walk away and never look back; that's your prerogative. I'm tied to you, but you aren't tied to me."

She stared at her hands as she wrung them in her lap, chewing her bottom lip before lifting her gaze to his. "What if I want to be tied to you?"

Warmth bloomed in his chest. "Then we'll be together forever. Here and in the afterlife."

"I'd like that."

The knot that had formed in his stomach when he found her fretting on the couch loosened. "So would I."

She traced her finger on his thigh. "And little baby Deaths? Can we…?"

"If you want to have children, yes. They'll be reapers. It's the only way more of us are made."

The doorbell rang, and Jasmine shot to her feet, wiping beneath her eyes and smiling. "That'll be Ella. Ready to end the pirate's rule of New Orleans?"

"You have no idea." He and Jasmine met her sister at the door, and Ella handed her an object wrapped in a dark brown cloth.

"This was his dagger. It's not in the best shape, so don't go trying to stab anyone with it." She cut her gaze between Jasmine and him, clutching her head. "Whoa. I'm trying to keep my shields up, but you guys are…" She pulled Jasmine into a hug. "I'm so happy for you."

"Thank you." Jasmine patted her shoulder before pulling away. "We've got work to do, so…"

"Oh, yeah. I'm leaving." Ella hugged Asher. "Take good care of my sister."

"I won't let anything hurt her." Well, nothing *else* anyway.

As Ella left, Jasmine unwrapped the dagger, cradling it in her hands. "This looks like a wedding cake slicer."

Asher eyed the knife, which did look like something that belonged in a bakery rather than on the belt of a notorious pirate. The teardrop-shaped blade was about four inches long, wide near the handle, tapered at the end, and inscribed with writing in Spanish. The dark brown bone handle was carved in the shape of a human head with ceramic eyes, and silver pins and twisted wire spiraled down the length of it.

Asher shuddered, recalling what a pain in the ass it had been to wrangle Lafitte the first time. Now, the pirate was unnaturally strong, and since he hadn't shown up in any of his other old haunts, he still had no idea what the specter was after in his escape.

"How do we do this?" Jasmine asked.

Resting one hand beneath hers, he placed the other on top of the dagger. "Use your magic to locate him, as if you were searching for any spirit. I'll try to amplify the signal for you, and hopefully together we can find him."

"Got it. Here goes nothing." She closed her eyes, inhaling deeply as a prickling sensation spread from her hand to his, shimmying up his arm where it burned in his chest.

"Your magic feels like heartburn."

"Wait for it…" The burning sensation cascaded downward into his stomach, settling there and turning into an electrical charge.

He felt her energy as she sifted through the remaining spirits until she found the one that matched the remnants in the knife. He'd never experienced anything like it. With his own power, he just sort of magically knew where to find the souls he'd been assigned to reap. Jasmine actively searched, and it was nothing short of awe-inspiring.

"Should I call him here?" She opened her eyes.

"No. I'll go to him."

"You feel where he is?"

"Yep. Got it." The Grand Terre Island. Rumor had it he buried treasure there long ago, though no one had been able to substantiate the claim. Perhaps it was true after all.

"When we get there, I thought——"

"I'm going by myself." He pulled his pen from his pocket and extended it into a scythe. He'd have to go full-on reaper—hellfire eyes and all—if he was going to catch Lafitte this time, and Jasmine couldn't be anywhere near him when he did.

She set the knife on the coffee table and crossed her arms. "No, you're not. We're a team, remember? Tied fates and all that jazz? I'm going with you."

"He's nearly killed you once. If it happens again, we're both doomed. Stay here. I promise I'll be back as soon as it's over."

If fire could have flashed in her eyes, she'd have burned the building to the ground. "Like hell. You—"

He didn't wait for her to finish her sentence. Instead, he slashed open a portal and jumped through, closing it quickly, before she could follow.

CHAPTER FIFTEEN

"That sneaky little soul sucker." Jasmine marched to the bedroom and grabbed the collapsible Faraday cage she'd created to capture the pirate. Asher *thought* he was going to end this alone, but that was horse manure. She just needed to figure out a way to get to the island.

Returning to the living room, she ground her teeth, eyeing the dagger on the table. Asher said he'd shared his essence with her. Did that mean she got some of his magic too?

"I wonder…" She snatched the knife and made a slicing motion through the air, imitating the way Asher opened his portals. Lafitte's energy vibrated on her palm, an image of his location forming in her mind, but the air around her didn't even shimmer.

She slashed again, picturing the place she needed to go, but again nothing happened. Grand Terre was a good hour drive away, and then she'd need a boat to get to the island. Asher could die before she got there. Did he forget he wasn't immortal anymore? She needed a portal, and she needed it now.

Grabbing her phone from the counter, she dialed Katrina's number. The succubus answered on the second ring. "What's up, girlfriend? I've got some exciting news."

"I need your help. Can you portal to my living room? It's an emergency."

"I'll be there in two shakes of an incubus's tail."

"Great… Do incubi have tails?" She waved the knife in an arching motion. Nothing.

"No, but they should. Filthy creatures, taking advantage of women like they do."

"Don't succubi take advantage of men?" She drew a circle in the air, attempting to make a wormhole. That didn't work either.

"I don't. Not anymore." The line went dead, and Katrina appeared on the sofa just as Jasmine whipped the dagger through the air again.

The blade passed inches from the demon's face, and Jasmine squealed, falling backward onto her butt, taking her small bookshelf and all its contents with her. Sharp pain shot up her spine as a dozen romance novels spilled around her, the bare-chested men taunting her. "Freaking phantoms! Sorry. Are you okay?"

"Oh, honey. I hope you're better at necromancy than you are at fighting." Katrina wore a tight red dress with a sweetheart neckline, and her dark brown hair flowed over her shoulders in silky waves.

As she rose to her feet, her image morphed, her hair losing most of its glossy shine, her voluptuous figure going from NC-17 to PG-13. "Using any kind of demon magic makes it hard to keep up my glamour. What's the emergency?" She held up a perfectly manicured finger. "Hold on. You had sex."

Jasmine scrambled to her feet, laying the dagger on the

coffee table. "How—" She clamped her mouth shut. Katrina's magic was founded in sex. Of course she could tell. "Asher needs my help."

Katrina's brow lifted. "Hate sex is my favorite. Do tell."

"It wasn't... Please. I'll tell you all about it later, but he's fighting a super-powerful ghost without me right now. Will you open a portal to Grand Terre Island so I can help him?"

"Another portal, Jazz? You're testing my limits today."

"I know. I'm sorry. If there were any other way, I wouldn't ask this of you. Please, Katrina?"

Katrina pursed her lips, narrowing her eyes as she crossed her arms and tapped her foot. Jasmine clenched her fists to stop herself from shaking the demon. Had she not expressed the urgency of this situation? Slow seduction may have been a powerful tool in a succubus's arsenal, but this necromancer was pressed for time.

After what felt like a thousand excruciating minutes, Katrina finally smiled and spoke, "Okay, I'll do it. But only because I love playing matchmaker, and I want to be able to say I had a role in your happily ever after with your reaper." She lifted a hand, her blood-red nails glinting in the light. "You don't want me to come with you, do you? I may be a demon, but I'm a lover, not a fighter."

"No, I'll go alone. But if you don't mind, could you take that dagger to Ella so she doesn't get into trouble at work?" Jasmine grabbed her Faraday cage that leaned against the wall.

Katrina shook her head. "I'll expect to hear all the juicy details and for you to start popping out baby reapers within the next year."

"If we make it through this, it's a deal."

"Have fun." Katrina sliced her nails through the air, opening a gateway to the island.

Clutching the metal contraption, Jasmine stepped through the portal, which instantly closed behind her. She moved to take a step, but her foot stuck to the ground like she'd landed in a massive wad of gum. The scents of decaying foliage and brackish water reached her senses, and she looked down, finding herself standing in the middle of a mudflat.

"Thanks a lot, Katrina." She'd have to have words with her demon friend after this was over. How was she supposed to look hot saving her man if she was covered in mud?

As she lifted her foot, the suction made an icky sloshing sound, and she cursed under her breath, lightly placing one foot in front of the other to avoid sinking. When she reached dry land, she spun in a circle, taking in the scene. Spanish moss hung like drapes from cypress trees, the afternoon sun filtering through, creating a dappled pattern of light and dark on the soft earth. In the distance, an abandoned fort lay crumbling from hundreds of years of neglect.

Asher and Lafitte were nowhere in sight. Did her friend even portal her to the right place? And of course, she left the dagger—her one way of locating the pirate—at home. Some ghostbuster she turned out to be.

"Well, Jazz, standing here isn't doing you any good. Go find your man." She hoisted the cage onto her shoulder, closing her eyes to feel the energy in the air. Any spirit vibration in this desolate place would probably lead her to the pirate, and as she sifted through the essence, a deep, menacing voice pulled her from her semi-trance.

She couldn't make out the words, and though the tone

was unfamiliar, her soul told her it was Asher. She followed the sound, her quick steps turning into a run as she burst through a clearing and found him.

He'd grown to at least seven feet tall, his formerly muscular body extending into a spindly, skeletal form. His dark jeans and black t-shirt had morphed into monk-like robes, the hood concealing his face and head.

He swiped his scythe, which had also grown to twice its size—did anything else double in length when he was in this form? *Focus, Jazz.* The fully solid ghost pirate disintegrated, reappearing a few feet away, laughing.

"You'll be marooned in Davy Jones's locker before you defeat me alone, ye scurvy reaper," Lafitte sneered. Seriously, could the guy be any more cliché? "Where is your necromancer?"

"Leave her out of this." Asher's voice had changed with his appearance, a low menacing growl replacing the smooth velvet cadence she'd grown to love.

"Avast ye, she's already in it, and I will collect me bounty." Lafitte turned his gaze on Jasmine as she clutched a tree trunk, rough bark digging into her hands.

"Jasmine," Asher growled. Her name sounded foreign and angry coming from the darkness in the hooded cloak, and she glimpsed a bony hand gripping the scythe as he turned away from her.

Now, at this point, she should have been terrified. At least a little bit scared. A super-ghost with the power to drain her life force in seconds was leering at her, while a giant skeleton with the ability to sever her soul from her body and ferry her off to the underworld was growling her name.

A normal person would've screamed, peed themselves,

and run—not necessarily in that order. But normal was something Jasmine had never been.

Was it weird she found herself attracted to the giant skeleton? Perhaps. Was it unhealthy that her concern for her own safety seemed to be nonexistent? Definitely. But worse than weird, worse than unhealthy, was the *stupid* thing she did next.

"Hey, Captain Morgan. Looks like you're *ship* outta luck!" she yelled as she darted into the clearing, headed straight for the pirate.

"Jasmine, don't." Asher focused on her, and in the split second he was distracted, Lafitte lunged, lifting Asher over his head and hurling him into the murky water.

"Better save yer boyfriend, lassie." The pirate winked, disappearing before her eyes as she ran toward the sandy shore.

Jasmine reached the water's edge as a spindly hand dug into the dirt. She gripped the sleeve of his robe, pulling Asher out of the water and rolling him onto his back. His hood slipped off his head, revealing the same skeletal face with blue fire eyes she'd seen when she touched his soul.

Tears brimmed in her eyes as she clutched his robe and leaned over him. "What were you thinking, dummy? You're not immortal anymore."

"You shouldn't have come. I didn't want you to see me like this." He turned his head away from her.

"See you like how? In your true form?" When he refused to look at her, she placed her fingers on his cold hard jaw and tugged his face toward her. "You're a reaper, Asher. I've always known what you are."

He sat up, finally looking into her eyes. "And you're not afraid?"

She laughed. "A necromancer afraid of Death? That

would be like a werewolf afraid of dogs. I'm not scared of you." And just to prove it, she planted a kiss on his lips.

Well, not exactly on his lips, seeing as how skeletons didn't have lips, but as she climbed into his lap and wrapped her arms around his bony form, he let her in, holding her tight.

"Is everything about you…" Now wasn't the time, but she couldn't help herself. She had to know, so she slid her hand to his lap and gave him a squeeze.

"I'm all bone, baby."

She grinned. "You certainly are. I love you, Asher, and from now on, we work together. Got it?"

"Yes, ma'am." He morphed into his human form while her arms were still wrapped around him, muscle filling out beneath his skin, the sinew returning to his body as he kissed her back. "I take it Lafitte got away?"

"He disappeared after he tossed you like a sack of potato chips. I've never seen a ghost with that kind of strength."

"It's suspiciously unnatural. I'm starting to wonder—"

A slow clap sounded from behind her, and she turned to find the pirate applauding them. She scrambled to her feet, clutching the pop-up Faraday cage, and sent out the biggest blast of magic she could muster. "Stop!"

Lafitte raised his hands in surrender. "Ye got me."

Asher stayed glued to her side, his scythe clutched in both hands, as she cautiously approached the pirate. Her magical hold on him felt secure, but he'd slipped from her grasp twice before. The odds were not in her favor.

She expected him to either bolt or attack the moment she got near him, but he simply stood there as she activated the cage and slid it over his head. She cut a sideways glance at Asher, who furrowed his brow, his jaw ticking as he ground his teeth.

"That was too easy." He jerked his gaze around as if waiting for an ambush. "What are you up to?"

"Nothing." Lafitte, floating in the center of his cage, reached a finger toward one of the metal rings, jerking it back when her magic zapped him. "This ole' seadog is tired and ready to return. I simply wanted a vacation like ye did."

"Let's go," Asher growled, hooking his arm around one of the metal rings and using his scythe to open a portal.

Jasmine stared in wonder at the door that lay on the other side of the opening—Asher's entrance to the underworld. Light seeping through from their dimension illuminated a tall, dark wooden door situated against a blanket of pure black. This was the gateway through which the spirit energy she called back from the dead passed, though she'd never imagined it looking quite like this.

"Has any living person ever seen it?" Her voice came out as a reverent whisper.

"Those who promise their body and soul to Satan see it on their way to hell." The portal shrank, and Asher swiped his scythe again, opening it wider. "Only one person has ever made it back topside after passing through it, and she had permission to leave from the Devil himself."

"Crimson?"

He nodded. "The immortal witch. Now, let me get this guy back where he belongs, so I can clean up the mess I made of New Orleans and your life."

"You didn't make a mess of my life. You made it better." She kissed him on the cheek and stepped back so he could pass.

He tugged on the cage, but it didn't move from its spot in the dirt. "The damn thing is stuck." He pulled harder, hooking his scythe around one of the metal rings, but still it didn't budge. "Did you use some kind of grounding magic on it?"

"No. It should move just fine." Jasmine gave it a shove, and it toppled over.

Lafitte slammed into the side of the cage, the contact sending an electrical jolt through his spirit form. Groaning, he floated to the middle of the space, rubbing his arms as if to rub away the shock. "I didn't sign up for this abuse," he grumbled.

"Well, if you'd have stayed put in the underworld, you wouldn't be in a cage right now, would you?" Jasmine grabbed a ring, and Asher helped her right it.

"Round two." Asher pulled on the cage, but he couldn't move it.

Lafitte crossed his arms. "Looks like ye have to work together if ye want to take me home."

Jasmine eyed the portal. "I can manage for a few minutes."

Asher shook his head. "That's the aether. You know what it does to you."

"I was in there for a good forty-five minutes last time. I can handle dragging him to the door and shoving him through."

Asher glared at the pirate. "If this is some kind of trick…"

Lafitte scoffed. "As if I'm known for me trickery. Ye can trust me. Ye have no other choice."

"He's right," Jasmine gripped the cage and slid it toward the portal. "It'll be a quick in and out. I promise."

Asher tapped his scythe against the bars. "It better be."

CHAPTER SIXTEEN

Asher kept a close eye on Jasmine as she maneuvered the caged Lafitte in front of his door. The pull to the underworld was stronger in this part of the aether, so she wouldn't be able to spend more than a few minutes on this side of the portal without going ghost on him. And that was something he would not allow to happen.

"Okay. You delivered him. Back through the portal you go, and I'll see you at home." He created an opening to Jasmine's living room and gave her a firm, yet gentle, shove toward it.

She resisted, taking his hand and squeezing it before crossing her arms. "I was thinking…"

"We don't have time for thoughts right now." He gestured to the gateway, trying to usher her through. Keeping the portal open for longer than a few seconds was draining. He needed to save his magic for opening the Devil-damned door.

She waved off his advance and moved toward the pirate. "I can move this cage without even touching it in here. Look." She lifted her hands, and Lafitte floated closer to the door.

Asher ground his teeth. With the pirate that close to the entrance, it should have unlocked on its own. His door should have sensed the pirate's energy and opened up to allow him back into hell. Something was wrong. Very wrong.

Jasmine continued, "I bet I can call the corral of ghosts to me. Just bring them all here at once, and then we'll be done with it." She arched a brow. "And then you can come home with me and celebrate…if you know what I mean."

He knew exactly what she meant, but he preferred to have her alive and whole when they celebrated. "Please don't. Just go home." His portal was slowly closing, so he ripped it open more.

"Look. I'm still solid." She lifted one leg and then the other. "I'm going to try."

He bit back a groan. "I have no doubts about your abilities. Your self-confidence is one of the things I love about you, but in this case, it's likely to get us killed. That cage was fragile at best. It might not hold."

"Too late." She grinned and gestured like a gameshow model as the magical enclosure, complete with the hundreds of spirits he'd trapped inside, appeared next to her, the foil balls clunking on the rocky ground when she released her hold.

The translucent sides bowed like a cartoon water barrel about to explode, and the ghosts moaned, a panicked frenzy forming inside the cell as some were drawn toward the entrance, while others tried to flee.

He didn't have much time before they escaped—or the energy to handle them all if they did—so he let the portal to Jasmine's house close and focused all his power on the door. Placing his palm on the grainy wood, he instilled it with his magic and tried the latch. It wouldn't budge.

He jiggled it and cursed, repeating the motions over and over, but the damn thing refused to give. "I don't understand why it won't open."

Lafitte removed his hat and fluffed the feather before returning it to his head. "Perhaps it doesn't recognize me essence because of the cage." He reached a finger to a metal ring, fisting his hand just before making contact. "I suggest ye set me free."

"Oh, hell no. That's not happening." Asher yanked on the latch again. Nothing.

"He's right." Jasmine stilled him with a hand on his bicep. "The magic in the perimeter is keeping his energy inside. We need to let him go."

"I promise to behave me-self." Lafitte's smile was alarming as he clasped his hands behind his back.

This was the longest Asher had been in his presence, and he raked his gaze over the ghost, taking in the details of his nineteenth-century clothes. He wore a buttoned waistcoat with a wide lapel, baggy trousers, and tall boots. There was almost a hint of color in the pirate's complexion, which was impossible. Ghosts were gray. Period.

"That's all it should take, right?" Jasmine's voice held a hint of panic. "If the door can sense him, it will unlock?"

He narrowed his eyes at Lafitte before focusing on her. "Yes."

"Let's do it, and then I should go home." She looked down, and Asher followed her gaze. The color had drained from her feet up to her knees, and she stumbled as she stepped toward the cage.

His heart dropped into his stomach, and he gripped

his scythe, ready to tear the pirate ghost in two if he tried anything. "Do it."

Jasmine gripped a vertical bar, unhooking it from the rest of the cage. Without the support, the contraption folded to the ground, and Lafitte stepped out of it. The pirate bowed formally, then placed a hand against the door.

A loud *clunk* echoed in the space as the latch disengaged, the hinges creaking as the door swung open. A blast of hot air from hell ruffled the pirate's feather, which was strange because wind didn't affect ghosts.

Asher's breath came out in a gush of relief as he turned to Jasmine. "I have to escort him through. Go home and rest, and I'll be there to take care of you as soon as I can." He opened one last portal to Jasmine's bedroom and took Lafitte by the arm. "Let's go, old man."

Jasmine turned toward the portal, and Asher stepped through his door with Lafitte. But before the entrance could close behind them, the pirate yanked from his grasp, and, moving faster than Asher had ever seen a ghost move, he grabbed Jasmine with one hand and a foil ball from the cell with the other, tossing the ball off the side of the cliff.

The cage disintegrated, and the ghosts swarmed, the pull of the underworld too strong for any of them to resist. They stampeded through the door, Jasmine getting lost somewhere in the fray.

Asher's blood ran cold. He couldn't see her. Couldn't sense her as the mass of spirits moved through the entrance and gathered on The Rock, where Charon stood waiting for them.

"Jasmine!" He searched, elbowing his way through the crowd, looking for her raven hair or a hint of her light brown complexion. It was a sea of gray. Cold and lifeless.

This couldn't be happening. He had to find her before Charon ferried her away.

"Reaper." The ancient man's voice sounded gravelly in his ears. "Come here, reaper."

"No. I need to find her." He shoved aside half a dozen more ghosts, but he couldn't see her.

"Come here, Asher." Charon's magic wrapped around him like a lasso, dragging him across The Rock to face him. His eyes were even more sunken in than the last time Asher saw him, and his skin looked like an onion. He'd never been an attractive being, but Asher's locked door seemed to have weakened the ferryman too.

Stretching out a gaunt arm, Charon turned his palm upward. "The tithes."

Asher tried to wiggle free, but the old man's hold was too strong. "There's been a mistake. You can't take her."

"The tithes." He sounded as if the entire exchange was about to bore him to death.

Asher reached into his pocket for the silver coins that magically appeared when he brought a soul into the underworld. As he dropped the handful of tokens into Charon's palm, they multiplied, turning from a dozen to several hundred in a blink.

"Asher!" Jasmine's voice cut through the commotion, and he caught a glimpse of her face as the spirits piled onto the ferry, taking her with them.

"She's there!" He moved to help her, but Charon tightened his hold.

"You're one tithe short," he said as he dropped the coins into his robe. "Someone doesn't belong."

"That's what I've been trying to tell you, old man. Jasmine is in there somewhere, and I need to get her out."

"Here she is, sir." Lafitte appeared at the edge of the ferry, dragging Jasmine out by the arm.

All the blood in Asher's head pooled at his feet. The chamber spun, and his vision tunneled before jerking back into focus. His beloved necromancer stood before him, not a drop of color left in her complexion. Her entire body had faded, transparency pulsing softly in her form.

"Jasmine." He ran to her, taking her in his arms and holding her close. She was cold and hard to the touch like granite. Like a ghost.

"Am I dead?"

He opened his mouth, but he couldn't respond. Instead, he glared at the pirate, white-hot anger flashing in his chest as he released his hold on Jasmine and stalked toward the murderer.

Lafitte held up his hands. "I did what I was told."

What he was told?

"Come here, child." Charon crooked his finger, calling Jasmine toward him.

Her feet didn't touch the ground as she moved to the ferryman, and when she stopped in front of him, she floated. Asher's entire world crumbled at the sight. This was his fault. Every bit of it. So scared of his fate, he'd run away from the one person capable of loving him, sending his life into a downward spiral that even her acceptance couldn't mend.

A vacation? He'd thought a vacation would solve all his worries? He deserved an eternity in the tarpits for what he'd done. "I'm so sorry, Jasmine."

Charon rested a skeletal hand on Jasmine's chest. "I'm afraid she won't be accepted in the underworld. Her heart still beats."

Asher's own heart soared with joy. If her heart still beat, there was a chance he could save her.

The old man leaned down and whispered something into her ear. She gave him a quizzical look, and then he shoved her through Asher's door, closing it behind her.

Asher lunged for the entrance, but Charon lassoed him again, dragging him away. Asher lashed out with his scythe, trying to break the magical hold, but the ancient entity simply laughed, shaking his head until Asher stopped struggling.

"She lives, boy. Calm yourself." He reached to the pirate and pulled him near. "I believe you have something that belongs to me." With a hand on the ghost's chest, Charon inhaled deeply, the small bit of color returning to his face as the ghost paled and became transparent. "Your job is done. Join the others on the boat."

"His job?" Asher shrank his scythe to pen form, shoving it in his pocket before crossing his arms. "Don't tell me you…" Charon wouldn't have. He couldn't.

"Of course I did. You weren't going to get off your ass and follow your fate otherwise."

"My fate." Asher scoffed. This was unbelievable. "You orchestrated this entire ordeal?"

"You were chosen, Asher. Your demeanor made you a prime candidate to bear new reapers. Why do you think you were assigned to Louisiana? Allowed to live topside in New Orleans?"

"Because I wanted to. I'm not a demon. I'm no slave to Satan."

Charon sighed, closing his eyes for a long blink. "You were there for *her*. Reapers capable of feeling such human emotions—of finding a mate—only come along every three hundred years. We are depending on you to increase the population, and you were failing us." He shrugged. "So, I stepped in."

"You could have just told me."

"Where's the fun in that? Besides, you are both stubborn. You had to come together on your own terms, or it never would have worked. Jasmine Lee was created for you, as you were for her. *She* is your fate. Go home to her. I will see these souls to their destinations."

"But she was a ghost. I barely saved her when just her legs went gray. I don't have the power to turn her solid again."

"I do, and I did. She's well. Go see for yourself." Charon waved a hand at Asher's door, and it swung open. "Your destiny awaits."

"That was weird." Jasmine rubbed her head and glanced around her living room. From her position on the couch, everything looked normal. The furniture was just as she'd left it, and the coffee table sat empty. Katrina must have taken the dagger back to Ella at the museum, but what happened between the time when Jasmine stepped through the demon's portal and now was a blur.

She crossed her legs, and dried mud flakes drifted down from her shoe. "That's right!" She'd landed in a mudflat on Grand Terre, and she'd found Asher trying to catch the pirate ghost on his own.

She gasped and held out her arms, sighing with relief when she found them flesh-colored rather than ash. Had she actually died?

Shooting to her feet, she strode across the room to the mirror hanging by the door. She pressed her fingers to her face and brushed a lock of hair from her forehead. "What the hell just happened?"

"Jasmine?" Asher sounded frantic, calling from the bedroom, and she rushed toward him, meeting him in the hallway.

"Jasmine." Relief filled his voice as he swept her into his arms, spinning in a circle and planting a passionate kiss on her lips as he set her down. With one arm on the small of her back, the other cradling her head, he coaxed her lips apart with his tongue and moaned into her mouth.

She clung to him, the fear she should have felt from the beginning finally catching up to her, making her tremble. She was shaking like a nervous chihuahua by the time he broke the kiss and pressed his forehead to hers.

"Are you okay?" He trailed his fingers down her cheeks before cupping her face in his hands.

She nodded, blinking back the tears that collected on her lower lids. "I guess bringing the whole mess of ghosts to the door at once wasn't the smartest move."

"No, it wasn't."

"I'll listen to you next time." As a tear dripped down her cheek, he wiped it away with his thumb.

"And I'll listen to you. From now on, we work together. Deal?"

"Deal." She led him to the living room and sat on the sofa. "Is it over now? Lafitte is back where he belongs, never to escape again?"

He let out a sardonic laugh as he sank down next to her. "Turns out, he never escaped at all. He was let out."

She gasped. "Let out? Who…?"

"Charon," he grumbled.

"The creepy old dude in charge of the boat?"

"The one and only. He charged up the ghost with extra power on his way out too."

"But why?"

"Apparently, I was screwing up my chance with you, and he thought we needed a little motivation to get together. He promised Lafitte an upgrade in his level of hell in exchange for creating chaos for us both."

"Wow." She leaned back on the sofa, shaking her head in disbelief. "All that just to play matchmaker."

"It seems we're fated to be together." He tucked her hair behind her ear. "We're supposed to help increase the reaper population."

"Oh, I see." She covered her mouth to hide her smile.

"But if you don't want to have a family with me, that's fine. No one is forcing you."

Her expression under control, she tilted her head. "Is now a good time to say I told you so? I feel like it is, seeing as how I told you we'd be good together right before I kissed you that first time."

He laughed. "Now is the perfect time."

She grinned and poked his side. "Told you so."

He wrapped an arm around her. "And you were right."

"You don't have to force me into anything. I've always wanted a big family, and if Charon meant what he said, we'll have all the time in the world to do it."

Asher tilted his head. "What did he say to you?"

"He told me to enjoy my immortality."

Asher's eyes widened. "Anyone who makes it to hell and back with their body intact becomes immortal."

"And since our fates are tied, that means you get your immortality back too."

His smile warmed her heart, and as he leaned down to kiss her cheek, she knew he would be all she ever needed.

All the acceptance and love she'd ever craved, she found in her angel of Death.

"I can't wait to spend the rest of eternity loving you," he said.

"Waiting is for losers. Let's start now." She climbed into his lap and kissed him.

EPILOGUE

"All caught up now?" Jasmine set a slice of devil's food cake in front of Asher and stood behind him, massaging his shoulders.

"Is this from Sweet Destiny's?" He angled his head to smile up at her.

She nodded. "It's your favorite, right?"

"It is, but her shop is all the way out on Magazine Street. You didn't have to do this." He sank the fork into the cake and took a bite, groaning with satisfaction.

"You've been working overtime rounding up the rest of the stray spirits. I thought you deserved a little break."

He laughed. "I'm never taking a break again."

"No?" She bent down, wrapping her arms around his shoulders and nipping his earlobe. "Not even to put a baby in me?"

He shuddered. "That's actually part of my job description now, so we can do that anytime we want."

"Oh, goody." She playfully bit his neck before straightening and pouring herself a glass of sweet tea.

"I do have one more spirit to reap," he said, "but I'm going to need your help locating him."

She leaned against the counter. "Cameron?"

Asher nodded and held up his phone. "He's the last one on my list, but since he's currently occupying a living body, I can't seem to find him."

"I think I may know where he is. Wanna portal me to the Garden District?"

"And leave my cake behind? I don't know."

She rolled her eyes, grinning. "He's a block away from Sweet Destiny's. You can buy a whole cake to bring home and eat on it for a week."

"I'm positive it wouldn't take me a week to finish it, but I will take you to the Garden District. The sooner I cross Cameron over, the sooner we can get started on the baby-making business. Let's go."

Sure enough, as Jasmine walked down the street, she found a woman in her early twenties sitting on the front porch of a lavender Victorian-style house and cradling an orange tomcat in her arms.

"Cam—" She started to call him by name but thought better of it. "Cam...per. Camper, is that you?" She stopped on the sidewalk and fisted her hands on her hips, hoping Cameron would get the message.

"Is this your cat?" the woman asked as she set him on the porch. "He's been hanging around my house the past couple of days. I hope you don't mind I've been feeding him."

Cameron rubbed his head against her leg before trotting toward Jasmine and letting her pick him up. "You dog," she whispered as she scratched his head. "Thanks for taking care of him. I'll have to get him neutered to keep him from running away again."

Cameron growled, and Jasmine laughed.

"No problem." The woman reached one arm across her body to rub the other. "I recently lost someone I cared about, so I've enjoyed the company. I have a dog, but your cat seems to understand me. That must sound crazy."

Jasmine smiled. "Not at all. Have a nice day."

As soon as she was out of the woman's earshot, she said, "Please tell me you didn't speak to her."

"I wanted to." Cameron put his paws on her shoulder to look behind them as she walked. "But listening was good too."

"Did you get the closure you were looking for?"

"I think so. She wasn't in love with me anymore, which deep down I knew. But she cared about me. That will have to be enough. Did Asher get his door fixed?"

"He did. Are you ready to go through it?"

"I think I am."

They met Asher at the bakery, and he grinned as he tucked a large white pastry box beneath his arm and portaled them home. Jasmine retrieved the ouanga that housed the cat's bitter personality and freed Cameron from the confines of his feline body.

Cameron's human figure floated in ghost form next to her, and he held out his hand to shake. "Thanks for everything, Jasmine. I'm going to miss you."

She took his hand, and for the first time ever, she didn't feel like her life energy was being sucked through a sieve. She could get used to this immortality business. "I'm going to miss you too, Cameron. Take care."

Asher took Cameron to the underworld, leaving Jasmine alone with the sleeping tomcat and his cantankerous soul.

"I suppose it's too much to ask that a week in an

ouanga tamed you, isn't it?" She blew out a hard breath and opened the jar, snatching the soul by the scruff of its neck and shoving it into the body like she was stuffing a teddy bear.

The cat blinked, looking around, dazed, and for a moment, Jasmine thought the ordeal may have subdued him after all. But when his gaze landed on her, he hissed, scrambling to his feet and swatting a paw at her before skedaddling off the counter and into the living room.

"Dammit, Mr. Puss." She gave chase as he darted through the house, bouncing off this wall and the next, knocking over her potted aloe vera and scattering the trinkets sitting on the end table.

"Oh, come on." She marched to the front door, throwing it open and shouting in her most authoritative voice, "Get the hell out of here, you pussy. And don't ever pee on my patio again."

The cat bolted out the door, and Jasmine started to slam it shut. But a squeal sounded from the porch. She opened it in time to see the cat climb up Katrina's front and leap from her shoulder before jetting into the bushes outside.

"What in hell's name?" Katrina dusted off her shirt and brushed past Jasmine on her way inside. "When did you get a pet?"

"Sorry. It's a stray I was trying to tame."

"I hope you're better at taming men?" She smirked.

Jasmine laughed. "Asher doesn't need taming. I like him wild."

"That's my girl." She pulled her phone from her purse. "Now, before you fill me in on all those details you promised me, I want to show you something." She swiped the screen. "My app is up and running, and people are signing up like crazy."

"What app?"

"I didn't tell you?"

"I've been a little busy lately."

"I created a dating app. It's like Tinder, but it's exclusively for supes. I call it 'Swipe Right to Bite.' Get it?"

Jasmine laughed. "I do."

"I was hoping to sign you up as a test subject to make sure everything is working properly, but I'm guessing that's out of the question now?"

"Yeah, I'm afraid I've got a standing date for the next thousand years, so…"

"Made it to hell and back, did you? Good for you." She pouted her lower lip. "Do you think Ella would want to give it a go? I know she usually dates humans, but for research?"

"She might… or you could do it."

Katrina scoffed. "Absolutely not. I'm fasting for my freedom."

"Nobody said you had to sleep with the people you meet. Just meet them. You never know… you might find love."

"Succubi do not fall in love."

Asher portaled into the room, and Jasmine smiled. "You don't know what you're missing."

ALSO BY CARRIE PULKINEN

Crescent City Wolf Pack Series

Werewolves Only

Beneath a Blue Moon

Bound by Blood

A Deal with Death

A Song to Remember

Crescent City Ghost Tours Series

Love & Ghosts

Love & Omens

New Orleans Nocturnes Series

License to Bite

Shift Happens

Life's a Witch

Finders Reapers

ALSO BY CARRIE PULKINEN

Spirit Chasers Series

To Catch a Spirit

To Stop a Shadow

To Free a Phantom

Stand Alone Books

The Rest of Forever

Bewitching the Vampire

Soul Catchers

ABOUT THE AUTHOR

Carrie Pulkinen is a paranormal romance author who has always been fascinated with things that go bump in the night. Of course, when you grow up next door to a cemetery, the dead (and the undead) are hard to ignore. Pair that with her passion for writing and her love of a good happily-ever-after, and becoming a paranormal romance author seems like the only logical career choice.

Before she decided to turn her love of the written word into a career, Carrie spent the first part of her professional life as a high school journalism and yearbook teacher. She loves good chocolate and bad puns, and in her free time, she likes to read, drink wine, and travel with her family.

Connect with Carrie online:
www.CarriePulkinen.com